LOVING EMMA

LOVING **EMMA**

By Alexis James

authorHOUSE®

AuthorHouse™
1663 Liberty Drive
Bloomington, IN 47403
www.authorhouse.com
Phone: 1 (800) 839-8640

Published by AuthorHouse 07/13/2015

ISBN: 978-1-4969-3147-4 (sc)
ISBN: 978-1-4969-3146-7 (e)

Library of Congress Control Number: 2014915050

TABLE OF CONTENTS

DEDICATION

For my husband and my two amazing kids....loving you is everything. I am truly the luckiest girl in the world.

"The bitterest tears shed over graves are for words left unsaid and deeds left undone." ~ Harriet Beecher Stowe

PROLOGUE

The casket is dark mahogany. The highly-polished, rich gloss wood glistens in the fall sun, making me once again grateful that I've decided to hide behind dark sunglasses. Large, yellow sunflowers are piled high on top of the lid; one for each of the few short years that she's been with us. Was, with us, I correct myself.

Twenty-six. She is...she was...only twenty-six.

I still can't think about her in the past tense, and I wonder if there will ever be a day when I can; when the thoughts of her won't rip all the breath from my lungs and steal every thought from my head. I knew her for more than half her life; but I've loved her since I first set eyes on her, back when we were in elementary school and I thought most girls had cooties.

Faith was different, even then. She wasn't into being the popular girl or dressing to impress anyone. She was always just herself; honest and brassy and balls to the wall, even way back in fourth grade.

I can remember the first time I met her, when my little sister Grace introduced us after school one day. She'd looked at me with those inquisitive green eyes and I'd been a goner. My twelve-year old self fell hard and fast, and even though it would take years for me to ever be anything to her other than her friend, I think I knew on that day that she would change my life forever.

She had, and did, in every possible and imaginative way. She'd been my enemy at first, as friends of little sister's usually are; annoying and always in your business...endlessly acting like she'd had the right to know every aspect of my life. Then at some point, maybe in high school, maybe before, we'd become really good friends. I'd give her advice on dating and the crap that guys would spew to try to get into her pants, and she'd nag at me not to be such a tool around girls.

Our love/hate relationship lasted until a few years ago; when my patience had finally run completely out and we were well-past the point of being just friends. The weird thing is, one day we were our normal selves, and the next we were....everything.

"Please stand."

I'm doing a fairly good job of blocking out the pastor's voice; this nothing of a man who never laid eyes on her before today. His words are just that; words. There's no meaning behind them, no feelings, no memories attached as he speaks about her. Those are all locked up in the hearts and minds of those of us who love her....loved her. Love her, I correct myself – yet again. I'll always love her.

"Stand up Liam," Grace whispers, her fingers digging into my arm. I comply, not because I want to; because what I really want is to crawl inside that coffin with Faith. Guaranteed no one at this service wants to hear me say those words aloud.

My legs are shaky and I feel myself begin to wobble unsteadily; the weeks and months of little sleep and excessive worry are finally beginning to take their toll. I feel Grace's arm around my waist; her vain attempt to hold my much larger body upright. Her strength amazes me and I wish I could reach inside of her and just borrow some of it. My own has been gone for a long time now.

I never considered before how empty I would feel with Faith gone. I swear there are times when I don't even feel my heart beating; don't really even feel like I'm alive, breathing in and out and blinking. I'm in that weird space between actually living and wishing I was dead; a place I could never tell Grace or my dad about because they'd instantly try to get me some medical help.

I don't want help. I just want to close my eyes and forget that this all has happened. I want to have her next to me, like she has been for the past sixteen years; the constant in my life and my reason to wake up and smile each day. Life without her in it is no longer filled with color; it's a gray landscape that I'll be forced to exist in because that's what I've been dealt.

The future we once talked about, planned for, and dreamed of is over. My future consists of getting through the next minute, the next hour, and the one after that. My future is gone, just as seamlessly as hers is too. Any hope I might have had for a bright, happy life died with her a week ago, when she took that final breath and I saw her life slip away right before my eyes. That last breath signaled the end of her life....and mine as well.

CHAPTER 1

MAY - 3 ½ YEARS LATER

My head feels like someone took a sledgehammer to it. And I'm fairly certain that if I move at all, I'm bound to hurl up the abundance of alcohol I ingested last night. I don't really remember anything that happened, though I do recall that it started with a party down the street from my apartment, and tequila was the drink of choice.

My eyes ease open when I feel fingers stroke the surface of my chest. Through my blurry vision I see a mass of matted blonde hair and a lot of bare flesh curled up against my right hip. My fuzzy brain informs me that there's an equal amount of bare flesh curled up on the opposite side as well; the owner's large breasts resting comfortably on my left arm.

God, I disgust myself completely.

"Um babe?" the one with the traveling hand whines.

I immediately toss her hand aside and pull myself into a sitting position; force myself to swallow back the urge to puke and try to shake off the dizziness. "I'm not your babe," I growl. I'm not her anything, nor do I ever intend to be. The only thing I am is getting out of here. Pronto.

When my foggy vision clears I realize that my problem is slightly bigger than the two naked chicks lying on either side of me. The two naked chicks are in my bed and in my apartment, and I've made a host of bad decisions. By the looks of things as I glance around at the scattered piles of clothing and empty booze bottles, this would qualify as one major fuckup on my part. I may drink too much, and I may screw most anything in a skirt, but I do not…ever….bring chicks back to my place. Obviously, my judgment last night was off. Way, way off. Obviously, I made some really bad…really poor….choices, as it were. The only thing left to do now is

1

to get rid of the evidence and forget last night…and these two chicks… ever existed.

Dragging on my jeans takes a monumental effort. Between the pounding in my head and the need to puke I'm minutes away from losing my shit all over my overnight guests.

"You need to go. Now." I'm rude and I know it. And quite frankly, I don't give two fucks. These chicks knew going in that they were getting one thing and one thing only from me. If I've done nothing else in the past three years, it's that I've perfected the art of being an absolute asshole. I have no trouble spelling it out to them; I want no strings - no conversation – hot, sweaty sex and if they're up for that, fine. If not, there's the door. I've yet, in the time that I've perfected this art, had any lack of female companionship.

"Now!" I snap, which rattles my sore head, but finally gets their fine asses in gear. I can't help but watch as they slide their perfectly sculpted… and medically enhanced…bodies into miniskirts and barely-there tops. Neither one of them is what I'd refer to as a beauty, but I do recall that they both knew exactly how to use those bodies to bring me the utmost pleasure. And really, that's all I could have hoped for.

The girls glare at me as they stroll by, although the one who has been silent the entire time does drag her fingernails across my crotch as a 'see ya later'. I briefly consider asking her to stay, then quickly remind myself that I've made enough mistakes during the past twenty-four hours and I sure as hell don't need to add to them.

An hour later my stomach is empty, I've showered and the sheets are in a pile on the floor. I briefly consider burning them, then remind myself that I'm probably just overreacting; and that a good hot spin in the wash will rid them of last night's filth. I just wish I didn't keep having flashbacks of me and the two blondes and for a minute I wonder if there's such a thing as a spin-cycle for my memory.

My phone chimes loudly and once I finally locate it under the bed I see that I've missed numerous calls from Grace. Before I can call her back she's pounding at my door and letting herself in with the key that I shouldn't have given her a few years ago.

"Christ!" she exclaims, pinching her nose with her fingers. "It smells like a brothel in here. What did you do?" Then she quickly throws up her hands and waves them in front of her face. "Never mind, I don't want to know."

I can't help but grin at her. Grace is not exactly Mother Theresa. "Well, I don't remember their names, but they had the finest..." I hold my hands up to gesture, just as she pokes her fingers in her ears and does her best la-la-la to block out my less than favorable words.

"Stop it Liam. I don't want to hear all about your smutty sex life."

I feign a perplexed expression. "What other kind of sex life is there?"

Grace rolls her eyes at me. "Enough already. Are we going to lunch or what?"

My stomach rolls at the thought. "Um, I might need to take a rain check on that sis."

She frowns. "Why? You drink too much last night? Again?" She says it with the accusatory tone she's developed this past year, when her tolerance for my alcohol consumption has dwindled as quickly as my consumption has increased. "You can't drink her away Liam. I know, I've tried."

Cursing, I flop down on the end of the bed and stare up at her. I know in my head that she's right. For more than three years now I've tried everything; drinking, not drinking. Sleeping, not sleeping. Eating, not eating. I've tried avoiding being with women, then sleeping with one after another to try to drive the images of her from my head. Nothing ever works. She's still there, as vivid in my thoughts as she was years ago; so tangible at times I feel like I can reach out and touch her.

"Are you okay?"

I know I'm frowning at her, and I know she understands why. I don't do pity; and neither does she. I rarely do the whole comfort thing actually, and the few times I've lost myself and completely fallen apart have been with her. Each time I walked away feeling like a pussy and a wimp. She understands the kind-of hell I live with every day and even though her relationship with Faith was different than mine, that doesn't mean she loved her any less.

Grace's blue eyes find my identical ones. "How about we forget lunch and drive out to the beach?"

For a minute I consider backing out, making up some dumb excuse that I know she'll see right through, but that she'll pretend like she believes because she loves me. And it's because of her resolve that I force myself upright. "Yeah, sounds good."

As has become our norm these past few years, we are silent as we drive; Grace's piece of shit car clanging and bumping along the freeway while her even crappier stereo garbles out music from our favorite station. I can't help but think about Faith; about how much she hated silence. She was always the life of any party, the one in constant motion and the voice that filled a quiet room. She emitted life from every pore of her body; from the long, wavy hair that she preferred to keep dyed a bright, vivid red, to the nervous energy that oozed from her and made it impossible for her to stand still. Faith was always going….always doing….always in motion - until cancer came along and robbed her of her spirit and zest for life…. and so much more.

Grace pulls into an empty spot and turns the engine off, but the car sputters a few times before it's finally quiet and she flings open her door. Her shoes are off and her pant legs are rolled up before I'm even on my feet and for a split second I swear that Faith has embodied my sister. Kicking off my flip flops, I take her hand and we move across the warm, white sand toward the water.

Faith loved the beach. She loved everything about it, from the salty taste it left on your skin to the grains of sand you were never able to get out of your hair. She liked to come here often, usually once a week or so. Sometimes we'd come during the day and bring a picnic. Sometimes we'd come at night, bring some beer, and find a secluded spot to be together. Faith was fun-filled, spontaneous and adventurous and more than once we had made love out here under the stars. I can remember how she'd laugh when sand would creep up into places it shouldn't; and tell me repeatedly that there will be no more fucking on the beach. I'd just laugh, mostly because I knew her; and I knew if she wanted me, she wanted me now, regardless of where we were. As she told me once, she'd waited a lot of years to have me all to herself, and she was never again going to wait to make me hers.

"Hard to believe she'd be thirty today," Grace says quietly.

"Yeah, I know."

Grace laughs. "Can you imagine that party?"

I laugh too; we are both well aware of Faith's driven need to party on her birthday. This one she'd actually started talking about back when she was a senior in high school, and I can still hear her going on and on about how people were going to be talking about her thirtieth birthday party for years to come.

I never thought, never even imagined, that just a few years after she made that declaration she'd be gone. I guess it just goes to show how submersed I was in her, in us. And how I took so very much for granted each and every day.

Grace and I walk along the water's edge, both lost in our thoughts; both clearly still raw even though I know we put on a good show most of the time. Grace is better at it than I am; of course I'm sure having Ryan by her side has helped. I wish I could say I wanted that for myself, but even the thought of letting someone in, letting someone close, scares the holy hell out of me. I know I'm young and I have my entire life ahead of me, but I seriously can't imagine anything more than the one night stands I've been embarking on since I lost Faith. Being any closer to someone than the few hours I'm in bed with them is really more than I can handle. As it is, I'm almost always so hammered I hardly ever remember any details. Unfortunately, last night's alcohol has not erased all the images in my head of the two blondes; those memories are vivid and much too unsettling.

We stay at the beach until the sun starts to fade over the horizon, then we load up and Grace pulls into the drive-through of a McDonald's and we grab some food for the drive home.

"You working tomorrow?" Grace asks, darting her eyes over at me while simultaneously shoving fries into her mouth.

"Yeah." My job situation has been laughable these past few years. I've pretty much job-hopped, unfocused and not nearly driven enough in one direction to need anything other than regular hours and a decent paycheck. For the past six months I've been settled into a job my dad got for me, working for a friend of his who owns a large construction company. My few years of college and steady employment since my early teens were enticing enough for the guy to offer me a killer position with this steadily growing company. I started out just doing a little bit of everything, but my incessant need to bury my grief in work has made me the perfect employee. I work ten or twelve hour days, five to six days a weeks, which leaves me little alone time to dwell or mope or drink myself into an early grave and a whole lotta time figuring out the ins and outs of the construction business.

I'm not gonna lie….I do give my moping and dwelling a good, valiant effort. And I've realized during the past year that my drinking has gotten out of control. I've also realized that the ghost of her is still here; and no amount of alcohol is going to make her go away. In fact, nothing will make any of it go away. The memories of what Faith and I had together are as clear now as they ever were. Unfortunately, so are the memories of her pain, her fear, her death. It is all inescapable.

I refuse Grace's offer to watch a movie or keep me company, knowing full-well that she understands my need to be alone. We share a long hug goodbye, then after I kiss her forehead and avoid the tears I see in her eyes, I head inside my apartment.

She's right, I think to myself, *it does smell like a brothel in here.* I quickly throw the sheets in the wash; drag out the vacuum and reacquaint it with the carpet that it hasn't seen in God knows how long. Then I dig around under the bathroom sink and find an old can of what Faith would laughingly refer to as 'poop spray'; give that a few quirts and hack and cough as the air is quickly scented with some flowery crap.

Flopping down on the couch, I glance around at the tornado that is my place. I've never exactly been Mr. Clean, but in the past few years I've neglected everything. I never do housework, rarely wash dishes and only do the laundry when I run out of clean underwear. I even stocked up on extra to drag my laundry chore out another few weeks. I'm pretty much your average single guy, a pig living in his own filth.

When Faith was alive she was here all the time, and it was nothing like the cesspool it is now. The place was spotless, the fridge was always full and yeah, it might have smelled like sex but that was only when we were really getting busy. It sure as hell wasn't the stench that somehow managed to linger from last night.

Christ, what the hell have I become? I used to be a decent guy. Even before Faith, I'd only slept with one other person. But since losing her, I've lost count of the number of women I've been with; and now that the twosomes have come into play I'm really batting a thousand in the morality department.

It's not like I'm professing to be some good guy. I'm free and I can do what I want. But I'm always left with this sick feeling in my gut after, like it's all just this side of sleazy; which is exactly how I'm feeling about the two blondes that entertained me last night.

My eyes are instantly drawn to Faith's picture; one of only two that I still keep out where I can see them. There are hundreds that I have - from our days as kids to those early days together as a couple - stacked in boxes in the closet. Knowing they exist is comforting; being able to look at all the minders of what can never be, continues to be more than a challenge.

This photo was taken the day I told her I loved her; out at our favorite spot next to the lake. I took it without her noticing; while she was staring off across the water, a small smile lighting her beautiful face. It was a perfect day. The most perfect day.

We wasted so much time dancing around one another; me afraid to tell her how I was feeling, and her uncertain and just so sure that I couldn't feel the same for her. Grace knew all along, probably from way back when we were kids, and did her best to try to get us together. Somehow we managed to figure it out all on our own, and for a very short time we knew what real happiness was.

When everything started to cave in around us – and cancer became our new enemy - we somehow managed to stay strong, still believe in forever, still have hope that maybe, just maybe, the diagnoses would be wrong. Even after the first round of chemo, the first surgery and radiation, we still held onto the belief that we'd have a future together; that all the time we wasted not being together would really be worth it…because we'd have forever. Right?

Faith kept that belief, that hope, right up until the end. And even when she completely lost the ability to speak, I could still see the resolve in her eyes. So I went out and bought a ring and I tucked it into my pocket and kept it there as a symbol of certainty that she'd come back to me.

I slipped it on her ring finger before they took her from me the last time; when the shell of the body lying in that bed was no longer the girl I'd loved since I was twelve. That girl, my girl, was gone now; lost to me forever and taking with her my future, our future, and any hope that I might have had that she'd come back to me.

I'll never regret buying that ring. I do regret every day not giving it to her sooner. I should have put it on her finger and married her that day by the lake. I should have made her my wife then, if not years before. I should not have spent years waiting and wondering and hoping that she'd be mine. I should not have ever hesitated to tell her how much I loved her; even if it meant doing so and getting rejected. Even though I know in the end she knew how much I loved her, and for how long I have loved her, I still regret not telling her earlier.

There are days, like today, when I wonder if that emptiness that I've felt since her death will ever go away. I have gotten used to it; gotten used to feeling nothing toward everyone except my sister. It's easy to feel nothing about a woman you pick up in a bar, and then use her body for your own gratification. It's easy to feel nothing about sex with strangers, because it's a space in time where thoughts and memories aren't required. It's easy not to be tempted to get close to someone, when I'm not with any one person long enough to even learn their first name. My life that used to be so full of love and promise is now one big unknown.

I'm not proud of the person I've become since losing her. She'd hate this new me and there are days I swear I can hear her, berating me with her non-stop bitching about how low I've let myself go. There are days when I tell the ghost of her that it's her fault I'm like this; her fault I'm left here all alone to pick up the pieces of my shallow life.

There are days....lots of them actually.....when I hate this new me too. I hate that I don't want anything, except my next drink and the next easy chick I can bang. I hate that I don't care about anything; not the cleanliness of my home, how I look or how I behave. I suppose I care about my job, as much as I have to to get the job done. And I do care about my sister, a lot. But my life could end tomorrow and I'd be okay with that.

I'd be with Faith and that's all I really care about any more.

CHAPTER 2

O nce June arrives, some of the fog that surrounded me for the month of May begins to lift. You'd think by now her birthday wouldn't rock me, and that each year without her would get easier. I don't know how it is for other people, but her birthday, for me at least, is just another reminder of yet another year without her. The only day that's worse is that day in October, when not only am I surrounded by the haze of grief, I usually spend the majority of the entire month drunk, pissed off and in tears.

Not a particularly pretty sight for a grown man.

June brings with it warm weather, long hours at the job site, and little time for me to spend on the sports of moping and dwelling. It's almost laughable to me sometimes; how much time I actually spend doing everything except living. Faith would hate it. She'd yell at me to pull my head out of my ass and move on with my life. And I'm sure this is what scares me the most. By letting go of my hurt and anger, I'll be letting go of her. I've held onto her for so long now I can't imagine not thinking about her every minute of every day. And there are days when I'm certain it's all driving me a little nuts.

June also brings with it Grace's birthday; something she used to celebrate with my red-headed dancing queen. Their co-birthday parties are still talked about in some circles; their twenty-first one for the record books. This year there's a party at Grace's favorite bar, one I've been to a handful of times. She's been grumbling about it daily to me; insisting that she does not want a party for her thirtieth and that she's seriously considering not going.

So, because of her repeated threats to me and everyone else about not showing up, Ryan has put me in charge of making sure she arrives at the party. It's not a job I take lightly; I know my sister and when she sets her mind to something it's fairly well cemented. I decide to head it off at the pass by showing up at her apartment just as she arrives home from work; catching her off-guard and well before she can have time to flee.

"I knew I shouldn't have come home," she grumbles, stomping up to her apartment and shoving the door open. She turns her angry blue eyes to me and glares. "You know I don't want this Liam. Why are you pushing it?"

I shrug and very patiently shut the door. "It's your birthday Grace. You should be celebrated."

She throws a few choice curse words in my direction, then resumes her stomping; this time across the room and into the kitchen. "What time do we have to be there?"

"Not until eight." I settle myself on her couch and take a look around the room that I haven't been in in months. Very little has changed since Ryan moved in before Christmas. Grace has a funky sense of style, so the place could easily house either male or female occupants. I do notice what appears to be a new Lazy-Boy chair, which I'm sure is Ryan's contribution to their joint space.

She hands me a beer and flops down on the couch next to me. "What's new big brother?"

I shrug again. "Nada. You?"

"Same. Work is busy, as usual."

I take a long pull on the beer. "How's it goin' with Ryan living here?"

Her eyes fill with light and begin to dance, and once more I swear I can see Faith in her. "It's good. Real good."

"That's great," I reply. *I hate you…and I'm so jealous.*

We shoot the breeze for a bit and then she calls out for pizza, which we both agree we will need considering that we plan on getting wasted later tonight. This is not news for me, but Grace's partying habits have lessened considerably since she and Ryan became an item. He's somehow managed to tame the beast in her and I silently wonder if I should thank him for that. I also silently thank the Gods that there's no one out there to tame my beast. I like my roar just fine the way it is.

After we gorge ourselves on pepperoni and olive slices, she heads into the bathroom to 'beautify'. I have ideas about what that really is, because Faith used to lay the same line on me all the time. Personally, both girls are knockouts so I'm not sure why it's even necessary to attempt to beautify.

Faith was a knockout, I correct myself.

I kill time by watching T.V. and helping myself to Grace's beer supply. When she eventually emerges from her bedroom, she's a polished version of the girl that left my side an hour before; dark hair a mass of curls down to her ass, some dark makeup around her eyes that makes her look somewhat slutty and also enticing at the same time.

Poor Ryan. He's gonna get eaten alive.

"All right," she states as she slings her bag over her shoulder, "Let's get to this shindig."

The bar is packed by the time we arrive and a big sign stating 'closed – private party' covers the entire door. We are immediately swallowed up by hoots and hollers and a very off-key and drunken version of happy birthday. Obviously, these guys started long before we arrived.

Ryan immediately shakes my hand. "Hey man, thanks for getting her here."

"Wasn't easy," I reply.

He chuckles and throws his arm around Grace's shoulders. "I bet not."

I head toward the bar, say hello to some of the people that I remember from my previous times here and take a seat on the last available bar stool. By the time my beer and two shots of Jack arrive, I've come to the conclusion that I'm probably gonna need to call a taxi tonight. Feels like it's gonna be a long one.

"Hey brother!"

I'm slapped in the middle of the back and it's a struggle not to choke on the whiskey I just swallowed. I glance behind me, see the massive sight of Grace's best buddy Moose. I like Moose….a lot. He's the type of guy who is easy to like, with his big, wide smile and friendly attitude. He's gargantuan, as tall as he is wide, and quite possibly outweighs me by two hundred pounds. But as intimidating as he can appear on the outside, he's just an old softy on the inside.

"Hey man, good to see you." I watch as he gives the guy next to me a shove, then settles his massive frame on the now empty bar stool.

He yells at the bartender to give us another round, then grins over at me. "So, you got her here. What did you have to use? Bribery, bondage?"

I laugh. "Nah. She came pretty willingly. After she threw a tantrum, or two."

His loud laugh booms out. "Don't they all!"

I hang out with Moose for most of the night, until his on-again, off-again girlfriend Autumn arrives. She's a cute little thing, and in another lifetime I might have been interested. But this new lifetime of mine leaves me not looking for permanent arm candy, but scanning the room for my next bed mate. The more alcohol I ingest, the bigger the need to squash the feelings about Faith; which seem at their worst when I'm relaxed and not on constant guard.

Ryan invites me to play a game of pool, and I gladly welcome the break from my inner turmoil. We talk about a whole lot of nothing while we play, and occasionally Grace sidles up next to him and they chat for a minute; or they spend more than a minute swapping spit. I really hate how I'm instantly jealous of my baby sister; jealous of her relationship, jealous that she's found a way to move forward with her life, while I'm stuck in this craphole with no way out.

"Having fun?" Grace asks me, her hand snaking down to cup Ryan's ass.

I grin at her. "Yeah. Not as much fun as you are, apparently."

She turns her drunken gaze up to the man that's glued to her side. "Oh, I have big plans for when we get home."

Another shot of jealousy slices through me. All I can hope to gain from tonight is a good buzz and hopefully a willing sex participant. "Good for you sis. Now get. Ryan and I have a game to finish." She staggers away and both Ryan and I start to chuckle. "I have a hunch her big plans are going to include riding the porcelain bus."

Ryan grins at me. "Uh, yeah. Got to agree with you there."

"Sorry man."

He shrugs. "It's all good."

We finish the game, and as usual Ryan wins, hands down. I re-rack for the next set and we're just getting started when a tiny dark haired gal greets Ryan. I watch as he gives her a brief hug and they chat briefly; sip my beer and try to check her out without being too obvious.

She's half Ryan's size, smaller than Grace, barely five foot if I had to guess. Her dark hair is pulled back from her face and like Grace's it hangs in a mass of wild curls down her back. From where I'm standing at the opposite end of the pool table, I can only see her profile; small nose, olive skin, and a rockin body that fills out the basic t-shirt and jeans to perfection. My pervy head instantly goes to all those places it shouldn't and for a brief second I ponder that she might be someone to consider as my next one-nighter. But that thought is instantly chased away when I see the way she interacts with Ryan; like they've known one another for a while and are good friends. I immediately cross her off the list. I don't do friends of friends. That just adds to the already toxic complications of the situation.

"Hey man, come meet a friend of mine," Ryan gestures to me, and he and the gal meet me half way. "Liam, this is Emma. She owns the coffee place that went in next to my shop. Emma, this is Liam, Grace's brother."

I glance down at her, and now that I can see her full-on I'm pretty much at a loss for words. She's beautiful; like cover of a magazine beautiful. Her eyes are large and shockingly dark; brown if I had to guess, but they appear almost black in the dim light of the bar. Her lashes are miles long and she's one of those rare girls who doesn't need to slather her face with piles of makeup; which is really nice for a change.

She greets me with a large smile, and holds out one small hand. "Hi Liam. Nice to meet you."

I grasp her hand in mine and immediately feel her touch race up my entire arm. Yanking my hand away, I shove it in my pocket and state, "Nice to meet you too."

"Grace tells me you're in construction," she replies, then sips from the beer that Ryan shoves into her hand.

"Uh, yeah. I am." Even buzzed, I'm tongue tied with this chick. It doesn't exactly make me happy.

"Cool party. Grace has a lot of friends."

I feel bad for her, she's really trying to pull me into a conversation and I'm just standing there with my head up my ass. But one look at her, one touch to her hand, and I can immediately tell that she's not the one night stand type; definitely not the type I need to be wasting my time with. Not that I exactly need those things as a reminder; her friendship with my sister and her boyfriend are quite enough to make me run in the other direction. "Uh…yeah."

Ryan frowns at me from his spot behind her. "So, Emma's shop is really cool. You should check it out sometime."

I swear I can hear the alarms going off; his blatant attempt to set me up with his neighbor more than obvious. In my head, I'm certain my sister has something to do with this too. "Yeah. Maybe."

Emma glances up at Ryan, then says, "Well, I'm gonna go find Grace. Good meeting you Liam."

I say nothing; not that I can't, just that I won't. I'm pissed off, irritated with my sister and Ryan; doubly irritated at this chick who I don't even know. Tossing down my pool cue, I drain my glass and set it on the nearest table. "I'm outta here."

"Liam, wait a sec," Ryan replies. When I stop, face him directly, he shoves his hands into his pockets and replies, "Look man, I'm sorry. Grace…."

"What?" I snap. "Grace thought that introducing me to some chick was gonna be the answer to everything?"

He shrugs, obviously uncomfortable. "I don't know what Grace was thinking. I do know that she likes Emma a lot, and they've spent some time together lately. I guess she hoped you two would be a good fit."

I shake my head. "Nope. Not happening."

He nods. "Yeah man, I get it. Sorry about that."

"Tell Grace goodbye for me." I shove my way through the mass of people, the need to leave the close confines of the bar pushing me forward. Luckily, I'm able to escape unnoticed and even though I have no business driving, I get behind the wheel and gun the engine.

I pull out of the parking lot and step on the gas; anger and pain clouding my head. Weaving in and out of the traffic, I barely make it through the yellow light before I cut in front of a slow car and peel the truck around the turn, taking it too wide. I don't have time to react as I slam into the parked car in the opposite lane; hitting it hard enough just at the right angle to send my truck airborne. I'm rolling, slamming around the cab and barely restrained by the seatbelt that I thankfully remembered to fasten. Just as my head pounds into the steering wheel and I start to lose consciousness, Faith's voice fills my ears; the echoing sound calling my name and begging me to come to her.

+++++++++++++++++++++

I can hear muted voices whispering around me as I try to force my eyelids open. My head is pounding and every tiny movement sends a slice of pain roaring through my entire body. Even the small, shallow breaths that I'm taking hurt like hell and for a moment I can feel myself falling under once again.

"Liam?"

I recognize the voice as Grace's and flinch when she calls my name again; this time louder, which instantly ricochets off my sore head. I hear a noise, which sounds like a moan and I'm fairly certain it's coming from me.

14

"Liam?" She's whispering now. "Liam? It's me Grace. Please wake up."

I can hear the terror in her voice; the raw fear that she hides so well and that I've only glimpsed a few times in the past. I try again, slowly force my eyelids open until I see her murky image looking down at me.

"Oh thank God!" she says loudly, and I guess I must flinch or something because she immediately apologizes and goes back to whispering. "I'm so glad you're awake. I've been so worried."

I blink a few dozen times and somehow manage to glance around slowly without it feeling like knives are slicing into my head. Along with Grace, Ryan is here, Moose too, and my dad and his wife Ruth are standing in the doorway talking to one of the nurses. I'm hooked up to an I.V. and my arms and hands look like they've been through a meat grinder.

"Liam? Do you know where you are? Do you know who I am?"

My eyes find her worried, tearful ones. "You're my pesky little sister."

She smiles at me and the tears roll down her face. "You asshole. I'm gonna kill you for worrying us like this."

"Please…do." I watch her smile fade and she turns away from me and falls into Ryan's waiting arms. Moose moves up to the side of the bed, his massive frame taking up one entire side and blocking my vision of my sobbing sister.

"Hey man, how you doin'?"

"Awesome," I reply sarcastically. I just wish everyone would leave so that I could go back to sleep; or wherever I was before I woke up.

"Need anything?"

Drugs, death….Faith. "No. I'm good. Thanks."

"I'm gonna take off. I'll check back tomorrow."

I watch as he engulfs my sister in his arms, then slaps Ryan on the back and makes his way across the room. He says a few things to my dad and stepmom Ruth, shakes their hands and then they move aside to let him pass. It's then that my dad's eyes find mine and even from across the room I can see the disappointment.

"How are you feeling son?" he asks, once he's standing next to the bed.

"Crappy."

He nods. "The doctors tell us that you were very lucky. You have a bunch of cuts and bruises and your head is pretty banged up, but you're lucky to be alive."

Oh yeah, I think to myself, I'm super-duper lucky. "Okay."

He frowns and his look changes from disappointment to anger. "What were you thinking? Drinking and driving? We've talked about this!"

He's right. We had talked about it…..back when I was sixteen and first started driving; a thousand years ago by my calculations. It's not like it's been a topic of conversation at the Thanksgiving table. "Yeah, I know."

Rage surges on his face. "You know? That's all you have to say?"

I should fight with him and really wish I had the energy to. But all I want right now is to escape into the oblivion I've been in for the past few hours…past few days….or for however long I've been in this hospital. "Yeah, I guess so."

"Dad, let's talk about this later," Grace interrupts, saving me as usual. "He needs to rest."

I watch silently as my dad takes Ruth's hand and walks out of the room; saying nothing else and leaving me feeling like a dumb-ass teenager. Grace takes her place at my side again and Ryan throws me a wave before he too exits the room. I'm positive my sister's been put in charge of reading me the riot act. Everyone knows that she's the only one I listen to these days anyway.

What I expect is anger. What I expect is disappointment and rage and her telling me all the ways I've let everyone down. What I get is a shaken, scared version of my strong little sister; as broken and beaten up as she was right after we lost Faith. Her blue eyes are awash with tears that stream in rivers down her face and even though my vision is still murky I can see that her entire body is shaking.

"Come here Gracie," I whisper.

She leans over through the wires and bandages and hugs me tightly; so tightly that I have to clench my teeth to keep from screaming out in pain. "God Liam, I thought I lost you. I can't lose you. I can't lose you too."

"You haven't lost me," I reply in her ear, though I think we both know that's up for debate. I've finally hit rock bottom and for a brief second I seriously consider staying there.

"You gotta stop Liam." She lifts her head, cups my face gently in her hands. "You gotta stop trying to cover your pain with alcohol. Look what's happened!" She stands upright and swipes at her face. "You're gonna lose your license. You may even go to jail. Can you tell me that's it's worth it?"

I can't tell her anything because right now I don't know anything. I don't know which way is up, I don't know how to crawl out of this dark abyss that I've let myself drown in, I don't know how to really smile again, or laugh again…or even consider loving again.

"Please Liam, if you can't do it for me, please do it for the memory of Faith. She would have hated seeing you like this." The tears start up once again. "She never, ever would have wanted you to waste your life being sad about her. She would have hated the thought of you being lonely." Grace leans down in my face. "You know I'm right."

Actually, I don't. Faith and I never talked about the after. Maybe we were in denial, or maybe we were so dead-set on hoping for a miracle that we ignored the reality that was right in front of us. But we never had that conversation; the one about me eventually moving on and having her blessing. We never talked about what her wishes would be for my future without her. We never talked about anything except our hope that she'd recover.

I suppose we were just that naïve to believe in forever. I'm sure that denial played a good part in that belief. And there are days I still find myself denying that she's gone; denying all that she went through and that she's no longer by my side as she was for most of my life. Denial works for me; most of the time. I guess it's what I've done since I lost her; deny her loss, deny my downward spiral, and deny that what I need is help.

I've been floundering for over three years; moving through each day, one after the other, existing on memories and alcohol and sex with strangers to get me through to the next day. And the one after that. And the one after that. It's no life and I finally realize that. But I truly have no idea how I'm supposed to rise above it all. Especially if doing so will mean letting her go for good.

CHAPTER 3

Two weeks later I'm finally able to go back to work. When I was first released from the hospital, I stayed with Grace for a few days until I was able to get back on my feet. The head injury that I sustained, even though I've been told it was relatively minor, still made me nauseous and dizzy whenever I stood up or moved too fast.

Grace doted on me during my stay; waited on me hand and foot and cooked for me constantly. I expected many repeat conversations like the one we had in the hospital, but she was oddly silent about my accident or the reason for it.

Her silence gave me a lot of time to think; too much, actually. I thought about what she said to me, how I've behaved the past few years, all the excuses I've used to act like such a complete ass. She's right; I have been using alcohol to cover my pain. I've been using it to feel better, to hide from my life, and as an excuse to treat people like shit. I've used it to get women into my bed, as a reason never to commit, and as my constant companion. In essence, I've become almost addicted to alcohol right before my own eyes.

This realization makes me physically sick. I've never been like this. Yeah, I might have experimented with drugs as a teenager and yeah, I've certainly done my share of partying. But never before have I used it for the cure-all for everything in my life. And never before have I had trouble walking away from it.

The day Grace drives me home and I head inside my crappy tornado of an apartment, the first thing I do is throw every bit of alcohol down the drain. It's painful and scary and more than once I'm tempted to just pour the liquid down my throat and say fuck it all. Luckily, I don't. Luckily, I have Grace's voice in my head and Faith's picture on my wall to remind me of how low I've let myself go. Luckily, there's just still enough left of me on the inside to know that I've got to at least try to make sobriety work.

The fallout from my accident has been massive. Like Grace predicted, I've lost my license. I won't have to serve jail time, but I will be required to perform a hundred hours of community service. The fine is a whole other story. I have no idea how I'm going to come up with the almost three grand that I owe, especially since getting to work for the next few months is going to be a challenge at best; my poor tattered truck has little hope of recovering. Makes me really reconsider my pledge to give up drinking.

Asking my dad for help is out of the question. He's barely spoken to me since his rant at the hospital, and even though I know he just needs a cooling-off period, I also know that his disappointment with me will linger. I've not exactly been the poster boy for an example of a guy with all his ducks in a row.

My first day back at work I arrive extra early, thanks to Grace and her insistence that she'll be driving me each day on her way into the office. The day is long, and my boss is less than thrilled with me having been off work for the past few weeks, but somehow I manage to kiss ass well enough that we move past the issue and get a few things accomplished.

Moose picks me up after a twelve hour shift and after we shoot the shit for a few hours over fully leaded soda and pizza, he takes off and leaves me with a pounding headache and a large pile of laundry that needs to be done.

For the next few weeks, my bevy of taxis gets me back and forth to work each day. In the mornings it's almost always Grace, but Ryan and Moose usually trade off in the afternoons depending on which one of them is available. On Saturdays it's a crap shoot, and by week three I've figured out the bus schedule and am managing to get there all on my own if one of my limos is unavailable. It sucks…big time…but as I remind myself frequently I did this; I'm in this situation because of the choices I made, and I'm just going to need to suck it up.

Surprisingly, my dad ends up paying the fine; of course, this is after he spends an entire Sunday morning berating me on the status of my life, how I need to grow up…blah, blah, blah. He's right, I know it. In fact, most everyone is right except me. I've made no good choices since losing Faith. I've hurt my family, hurt my body, and lost any morals I might once have had. Rebuilding all that is going to take time and energy; energy that I don't really believe I have.

Week four and I'm seriously starting to go nuts not having my own transportation. It's Saturday and luckily I don't have to be to work until ten, so as usual I'm waiting for the honk outside; my charity ride to the site. I'm grumpy and sleep deprived; my lack of alcohol is wreaking havoc with my ability to actually sleep. Now I remember why I started drinking in the first place.

Grace is my token chauffer today and greets me with a sleepy 'good morning' before we set off down the road. I'm silent, staring out the window as she drives along, not even realizing that she's driving in a different direction than she usually does when she's hauling my ass to work. It's not until we pull into the parking lot of Ryan's tattoo shop that I finally get a clue that we're making a stop before she drops me off.

"I need coffee," she states. "Come on."

I follow along, mostly because I too could use some caffeine. My vehicle restriction of the past month has made grocery shopping almost impossible, and since I've mostly been existing on whatever takeout that can be delivered and my cupboards are bare, coffee has been a hit or miss luxury.

We head to the tiny shop next door to Ryan's with the purple and white striped awning and large logo painted on the inlaid glass of the front door. A small bell jingles as we head inside and I'm immediately assaulted with the strong smell of coffee, followed by the mouth-watering scent of homemade pastries.

Grace strolls up to the counter and peers into the large glass case. "God, I want one of everything."

"Can't. Cuz then you'll be bitching about how they all went right to your ass."

She turns around and smacks me in the center of my chest. "You're such a dick Liam."

I shrug. "Yeah. But I'm right."

"Hey Gracie!"

My eyes quickly find the owner of the sweet sing-song voice and the instant I recognize her, my first instinct is to flee. Emma is just as beautiful in the light of day as she was in that dingy old bar over a month ago; more so probably, especially now that I can see her dark mocha eyes shining with life. Her dark hair is piled into a bun on the top of her head, giving her the illusion of being taller than she actually is. There's a smudge of flour on one cheek and a smear of what I think is chocolate on her neck.

The fact that I want to lick it off doesn't escape me.

"Hey Em! How are you girl?"

Emma shrugs. "Busy, as usual. Thank God." Her eyes travel up to meet mine. "Hi Liam." I give her a head nod, but I couldn't talk even if I wanted to. She seems to take it in stride and turns her attention back to Grace. "So, what'll you have?"

Grace rattles off her order for coffee, chooses a few items from the pastry case and keeps up a running conversation with Emma while her coffee is prepared. I stand there like the idiot I am, watching the way she moves so quickly and efficiently; her small hands mastering the large cappuccino machine like that of an expert barista.

"What can I get you?" she asks me once she turns back around.

"Coffee. Black."

She nods, then goes right back to chatting with Grace as if I'm not even in the same building. I guess I should be grateful. She has obviously dismissed me as quickly as I have her. By the time she slides my cup across the counter and rattles off an amount, I'm anxious to get out of this cozy space and as far away from her as I can get.

"I need to get to work," I tell Grace as I head for the door. By the time she joins me outside a few minutes later, I'm pissed at her for dawdling and I'm convinced she's pissed at me just for being me.

"Could you have been any more of a dick to her?" Grace snaps, shoving the car into reverse and peeling out of the lot.

"I need to get to work," I repeat. My excuse is lame, but I don't really want to get into this with my sister. I have no idea why I keep reacting to Emma the way I do.

"You are an ass, you know that?"

"Actually, yes I do."

Grace darts her eyes at me. "She's a nice person Liam. She's a good person. It wouldn't hurt you to be kind to her."

"Knock it off Grace."

"But Liam, she is…"

"Enough!" I growl. "Just leave it the fuck alone."

"Fine."

I hate when women do that; when they say "fine" and mean just the opposite. Things aren't fine….she isn't fine with my decision to blow off Emma….there's nothing fine about this whole fucking situation. Life is not fucking fine!

By the time she drops me off at work, I'm seething and she won't even look at me. I don't like arguing with my sister, but I don't know any other way to get it through her thick skull that I have no intention of getting to know Emma. Twice now I've been around her and both times I've felt off-kilter and upended just being near her. Life is easy when I'm around women who make me feel nothing but pure primal lust. Lust, I know; lust, I'm comfortable with. I'm not saying I don't feel a tug of that toward Emma; obviously I must if my first instinct was to lick the chocolate off her neck. But I don't need the confusion of someone like her...someone good and kind....in my life. Frankly, all I need is willing and semi-slutty. Gross, but true.

+++++++++++++++++++++

I finally get my license back a few weeks later, but my poor truck isn't even drivable. Moose has been working on it a little at a time, whenever I can fork over some cash for the repairs, and I know he's been doing a bunch of stuff for free too. Not a bad thing to have a friend who is a mechanic, that's for sure. He's currently looking for tires, has a radiator waiting to be installed and then he says I'll at least be able to drive myself back and forth to work.

Thank you....thank you....thank you....

So it's another Saturday morning and even though Grace and I are back on speaking terms I can instantly tell that we are making yet another pit stop on her way to take me to work. I say nothing this time, mostly because I really hate arguing with my sister and also because I really could use another cup of Emma's amazing coffee.

Once we're parked, she flings open her door, and I request, "Bring me a large coffee, will ya?"

She stares at me for a good long time, then rolls her eyes and shakes her head. "Nope. If you want coffee, get it yourself." Before I know it she's stomping off toward the café, long hair streaming behind her in the warm summer breeze.

Swearing under my breath, I follow her inside and actually take a minute to glance around at the small, quaint space. There are five or six small tables, all painted white, with fully padded chairs covered in a vibrant purple material. The "Bella Café" logo is emblazoned on the back wall and the décor is simple with a few black and white pictures lining one wall and a large plant filling one corner. The glass pastry case and counter line the opposite wall, and it's there that Grace is once again standing, talking a mile a minute with Emma.

This is the Grace I used to know; back when Faith was alive and she was free to be herself. She was fun back then, free, animated like she is now; not angry and so lost inside herself that she made it difficult for anyone to want to be around her. It makes me wonder how Ryan found a way in, and Moose too for that matter. Then I realize that they both really love her, and I guess for real love you'll do anything. I know I did once.

"Coffee, black?" Emma asks once I reach the counter. I nod, silent as usual. I'm a real charmer, obviously.

Grace sips at her coffee and watches me out of the corner of her eye, but wisely keeps her mouth shut. I murmur my thanks to Emma when she slides the tall cup across the counter, and slap some money down before she can rattle off the amount.

I'm at the door, pulling it open when I hear her call, "Your change!"

Grace, who is standing behind me, turns to Emma and says, "Keep it. You've earned it."

For the next two Saturdays we repeat this same trip. I say nothing, Emma keeps my money and Grace spends a good amount of time laughing at me but not actually saying anything. When Moose calls and says my truck is back up and running I'm oddly disappointed that my Saturday morning coffee stops will now be coming to a halt.

I try telling myself it's because I'll miss the great coffee, but the annoying voice in my head that appeared right after I stopped drinking tells me that there are a variety of reasons that I'll miss stopping by; least of which is the coffee. I'm sure it has nothing to do with the fact that I like watching Emma move; that no-nonsense way she has to multi-task and make it all look so easy. I'm sure it has nothing to do with those large, inquisitive dark eyes that say more to me than any words ever could. And I'm certain it has absolutely nothing to do with the fact that she constantly has something edible on her face or neck; calling up all kinds of indecent images in my head each and every time.

So when Saturday morning rolls around and my truck just happens to drive itself toward the café, I'm fairly certain I've either lost my mind completely, or I'm just that dead set on making my life as miserable as it can be.

I'm earlier than usual and because of that I'm the only one in the shop. Soft music plays over the speakers that hang from two corners of the ceiling and I'm positive I recognize it as an opera Ruth dragged us to as kids. I hear a voice call out, "Be right with you!", so I head to the pastry case and try to decide what to splurge on.

"Sorry about that. How can I…." Her eyes find mine as she moves into the front room and I notice how her expression goes from friendly to nondescript in less than a second. "Coffee?"

I nod. "Yep. And I'll take one of those tortilla things with the filling."

She chuckles and pulls a small paper bag from under the counter. "It's called cannoli."

"Yeah, a cannoli." I watch as she leans into the case to extract my item, then ask, "They any good?"

She raises one dark eyebrow at me. "Of course they're good. I made them."

I can't help but smile at her. "Well, how about you let me decide."

She says something under her breath and hands me the bag, then turns back around and starts to fill my cup. I pull out the pastry and bite into the flaky crust. The sweet, creamy filling hits my tongue and explodes with flavor and I hate to admit that she's right; it's good…really, really good.

Emma sets my cup on the counter and folds her arms across her ample chest; glaring at me as she rattles off the price. I lick my lips and set the remaining portion of the pastry back in the bag; force myself not to have her give me at least five more, they are just that decadent.

I yank out my wallet, slap some bills down on the counter and pick-up my coffee. "Thanks."

I'm almost at the door when she calls out, "Aren't you gonna tell me what you think about the cannoli?"

Turning to face her, I grin and reply, "Nope. See ya." I'm quite certain I hear the word 'asshole' just as the door slaps closed behind me.

+++++++++++++++++++++

Emma

Since I was a little girl I've dreamed about owning my own bakery. I'd bake with my Nana, let her teach me all the ins and outs of proper Italian baking, and keep all my notes and information written in a three-ring binder that to this day I keep on a shelf in the kitchen.

That binder has all the family secrets in it; like how much lard to use to make the perfect biscuits, to the secret ingredient in Nana's gravy (Italian for spaghetti sauce). My first sketch of the café logo is in that binder, along with my business plan (written at the ripe old age of twelve), menu mock-ups and page after page of layouts of the actual space itself. On paper it looked good; in person it looks amazing. It's taken me a long, long time to see this come to life and even after being in business for the past five years, moving to this new location was really terrifying. I have a good, steady stream of regular customers, many from the surrounding businesses, and with a new marketing plan in place I'm finally beginning to reap the benefits of all my hard work.

My mom is on me constantly....how are you going to meet a husband when all you do is work? When am I ever going to have grand children? And on and on and on. I'm literally on repeat when I tell her that I have no intention of meeting a husband; I'll be lucky to meet a guy I want to date more than once. I have no time for kids, now or in the foreseeable future. And then I remind her to bug my brother Mario; he's the one with the wife and the baby on the way.

Meeting Ryan and Grace has really been a godsend. I work so many hours that I don't have time for friends, let alone any kind-of personal life. Being the owner and the only person who does all the baking, requires me to practically live here at the café. Having them stop by and chat fairly frequently, helps me greatly in not feeling like the hermit that I've become.

Grace and I have become close these past months, and often she'll stop by after work and help me out in the kitchen while she waits for Ryan to close up the tattoo shop for the day. I like having her around, and the extra set of hands is nice too. Grace is new to the art of baking, but she's willing to learn and asks a ton of great questions. I haven't told her yet, but I could really see her working here with me on a permanent basis. Then I have to remind myself....by having Grace around more that will mean her tool of a brother Liam will be around more too.

I don't get him; at all. I've only ever been nice to the guy and he's only ever been rude to me. I tried asking Grace about it once, but she just mumbled some bull that sounded convincing to her but not to me; and then she skedaddled back to Ryan's shop. I haven't mentioned it, or him, since. In fact, I don't really want to talk about Liam at all. He's rude and arrogant and what do I care if he's drop dead gorgeous.

Oh my gosh…he is so gorgeous! With that shock of black hair, those big blue eyes and that chiseled jaw….I literally feel like a puddle at his feet whenever he looks at me; which I'll admit, isn't often. I do sometimes catch him checking me out when he thinks I'm not looking, but mostly he avoids looking or talking to me. He's not a big guy, more the long and lanky type, but he towers over me and he sure fills out a pair of jeans nicely.

Not that I've noticed. I haven't. I don't notice those things. I don't have time to notice things like a great looking ass or wide shoulders that were made for my hands or lips that are just soft enough to nibble on.

I do not have time to think about asses or shoulders or lips. Sadly, I can't even remember the last time I saw a man without clothes on, let alone the last time I was kissed. All my life I've been driven to get my café off the ground. I've had one sole purpose and I've never let anything get in my way. And now that the café is up and running and so far is successful, I have even less time to think about what I want for my future. My future is about coffee and pastries, not hunky blue-eyed guys. Period.

CHAPTER 4

The following Saturday I'm up early, though I refuse to admit to myself that it's because I'm anxious for my coffee stop. I also refuse to admit that I've done nothing but think about Emma all week; or that I had a dream about her two nights before.

I completely refuse to admit that the dream was anything other than G rated.

My frustration over this non-situation with Emma, my lack of anything alcoholic and my complete halt to all sleazy bed partners has made me a pretty grouchy guy. Luckily, at work I'm busy and push myself so hard physically, there's no time to spend feeling sorry for myself; which I will finally admit I've done a lot of these past few years.

I do, however, take my grouchiness out on those closest to me; namely my sister. As of last night, when I snapped at her one to many times, she informed me that she isn't speaking to me again until I get laid. I'm positive I'm not speaking to me or anyone else either until I get laid; I'm just that obnoxious.

So, after Grace hung up on me I decided to put a plan into action. It would have to be alcohol free; not because I'd want it to be but because it is necessary. I scrolled through my phone, picked out one or two prospects and made a few calls. Hopefully tonight my grouchiness will end, even though it's gonna cost me an expensive dinner out.

There are two people standing at the counter when I arrive at the café thirty minutes later. While I wait, I watch Emma interact with the customers; her charming, friendly attitude and easy laugh such a change from the woman I usually deal with. Of course, I remind myself silently, I do happen to bring out the worst in her. It's not like I'm exactly a nice guy.

Once the two people are situated, I move up to the counter and her smile instantly fades. "Coffee?"

I nod. "Yep. And one of those tortilla things." I glance at the case. "Throw in one of those little things with the chocolate on top too." I gesture with my finger when she moves into my vision behind the glass.

As she slides the pastries in the bag, she replies, "It's cannoli. And the little thing is called a zeppole."

"Yeah, okay. Whatever." At this point I'm trying to piss her off, and I really wish I knew why; except that I do enjoy seeing those big brown eyes of hers fill with fire.

While her back is to me at the coffee machine, I assess her tiny figure. Like all other mornings, she's wearing a purple t-shirt with the café logo splashed across her chest, a splattered apron tied at her waist and well-worn jeans. Her ass is just the perfect size to fit in my hands and I immediately have to push the image aside and attribute my horniness to lack of female companionship for the past few months.

She turns back around so quickly that I'm sure she knows I was checking her out; but I feign nonchalance and reach into my pocket for my wallet. "How much?"

"I'll tell you when you tell me why you were looking at my ass."

Caught off guard by her direct hit, I can't help but laugh. This chick has my balls in a vice grip, that's for sure. I shrug and toss some bills down onto the counter. "You've got a nice ass." I pick up my coffee and bag of goodies and head toward the door. "Keep the change. You've earned it."

"You're a jerk!"

"Bye Emma. Have a nice day," I laugh, shutting the door behind me.

The entire time I'm working I can't get our conversation out of my head. I don't want to, but I like her. I like her no bull-shit style and the fact that she doesn't take any of my crap. I like that she's not charmed by me, like so many flighty chicks are these days. In fact, I wouldn't be surprised if there are times I mostly disgust her.

So obviously my head is not into my date later that night, even though my date, Jenny, does her best to keep me entertained. I'm cordial, and I do contribute what I can to the conversation, but what I really want is for her to shut up and for us to get things moving.

Yeah, I'm an asshole of epic proportions all right.

Two hours later things are moving. I'm buried deep inside her, her nails are tearing down my back, and she's already come twice. I, however, am having a hard time staying focused on the woman under me; especially when it's a certain other woman's face that I keep seeing in my head. I finally have to close my eyes; pretend it's her lying under me, calling out my name and begging me not to stop. I pretend it's her hands grasping at me, her legs wrapped around my waist. I pretend it's her ass my hands grip as I pound faster and harder and deeper each time.

I feel her tense underneath me, the deep moan as she lets go and I finally slide into oblivion with her, growling out, "Ah fuck…Emma…."

++++++++++++++++++++

Suffice it to say, Jenny and I won't be seeing one another again. Upon my very vocal release of another woman's name, she shoved me off her and immediately ordered me out of her apartment. I headed home, satisfied and spent; and thoroughly and completely disgusted with myself. Again.

This isn't the first time I've been with someone and been thinking about someone else. But usually, that someone else is Faith. In fact, I don't think I can remember a time where I've been with someone and not thought about Faith; until tonight. I'm not sure if I should feel guilty, repulsed or just simply glad that I've seemed to finally be able to move past that hurdle.

Now however, I have this new obstacle to deal with. I have no business thinking about Emma in that way. And I sure as hell have no business thinking about her while I'm inside another woman. That's just wrong.

I take this as my cue to stay away from her. Nothing good can come from my visits to her café. Yeah, I'll miss her amazing coffee and pastries, but knowing that I won't have to go through again what I experienced tonight will be worth it.

The next few weeks at work are long; but the Saturdays are brutal. I refuse to admit to myself that it has anything to do with the fact that I'm missing that amazing coffee and those mouth-watering pastries. I sure as hell refuse to admit that it has anything to do with *her*. I've yet to go one day without thinking about her, which just royally pisses me off, and by Saturday evening I'm itching for my usual; a good buzz and an even better lay.

I meet up with Moose at the bar and begrudgingly order a soda before we rack the balls and start playing pool. He's a good distraction from all my inner turmoil; keeping me laughing about everything in general and telling me one story after the other about something crazy he's done. I'm on soda number two when I notice Grace and Ryan walking through the door, followed immediately by a certain dark-haired lady that's kept my head occupied for the past few weeks.

They make their way straight toward us and after greeting Grace with a hug and Ryan with handshake, I give Emma a head nod and say hello. This time I notice, she says nothing. As a group, we decide to team up and play pool; me and Ryan against Moose and the girls. I'm not sure how he ends up with them, though I could guess it has something to do with his massive amount of flirting. As we play I watch he and Emma together; see how freely he puts his hands around her small waist to show her how to hit the ball or how she smiles so beautifully up at him. Me, she ignores completely.

After the game I head to the john, and upon my return I stop by the bar and toss back a few shots. When I'm back at the pool area, I'm told that new teams have been chosen. Moose informs me that it's he and Ryan and Grace against me and Emma. I notice how quickly she and I both start to protest, and also how quickly the three of them ignore us.

Resigned, I gesture with my pool cue to her. "Ladies first." She just rolls her eyes at me and leans over the table. It takes super human strength not to stare at her ass.

The three idiots on the other team spend a whole lot of time wasting time between shots and generally drawing out the game as long as possible. By the time Moose makes a second trip to the bathroom, both Emma and I are on to them and have somehow managed to start working as a team instead of the strangers that we are.

"What's going on?" she asks as we stand huddled in the corner at the opposite end of the table from my ex-sister and my ex-friends.

I shrug. "Shitty attempt at matchmaking, I think."

She rolls those big, beautiful eyes and glances up at me. "It's not gonna work. You know that, right?"

I snicker. "I knew it back when I first met you. They just don't know how to take a hint."

Her eyes find mine again. "Well, we could pretend like it's working. Maybe they'll back off."

I consider her request; feel it center right where it shouldn't in my jeans. "Pretend how?"

She shrugs. "I don't know. Flirt a little, I guess. Make googly eyes at one another."

I laugh. "What the hell are googly eyes?"

She starts to laugh. "I don't have any idea. I heard it in a movie once."

I take a step closer. *Twist my arm.* "Okay with me. Googly eyes it is." My fingers trail down her cheek and for a second I can tell that the three stooges all stop talking. For a minute I briefly consider that this sure as hell doesn't feel like anything fake to me. "I think it's working."

She nods once. "Um…yeah…me too." Her small hands wind up, center on my chest, then slide around my neck.

I feel the touch of her hands like a lightning rod over my entire body and immediately pull her closer until our bodies are nestled together. My eyes roam over her exquisite face, to her plump pink lips that are practically begging to be kissed. And when she darts out her tongue to wet the surface, it takes every ounce of restraint that I have not to lean in and capture her mouth in mine.

My whole body is reacting to her, to her closeness, to her touch. My heart is racing in my chest, with anticipation….with fear maybe. And there's not one part of me that doesn't feel the effect of her body up against mine, her touch bleeding into my veins. The feeling is so foreign….so different from the normal reaction I have to women, which is usually just a big surge of lust, followed by a whole lot of nothingness. Yeah, there's lust here too; in spades. But the emptiness I've felt before….felt for years now, is suddenly and miraculously gone.

Instantly, Faith's face flashes in my head; and the feeling of betrayal and disloyalty hits me square in the chest. Immediately, my ability to actually take a breath is a struggle, something forced. My reaction is instantaneous and like Emma's touch I feel it throughout my entire body; a chilling cold ice that spreads from my hands that are around her waist all the way down to my toes.

I'm not sure what she sees on my face, but the frown and look of concern are enough to spur me into action. I quickly set her aside, none to gently I might add, and say something incoherent before I head toward the door. I hear voices behind me, calling out my name, but I'm on a mission to flee; to get as far away from everything and everyone as quickly as I can.

I somehow manage to get to my truck, crawl inside and gun the engine before Grace or Ryan or Moose can reach me, though I do see their mutual looks of concern and hear Grace scream for me to call her as they head in my direction. I know she knows that I won't; not until I can.

Like the drunk I used to be, I weave my way home without actually being conscious of the drive itself. And like that person I once was, I'm seriously jonesing for another drink; anything to chase away the demons that seem to all have pushed to the surface all at the same time. I force myself past the liquor store that calls out to me loudly and obnoxiously and finally manage to make it home.

I'm shaking from head to toe by the time I walk through my door. My phone is blowing up in my pocket, and without glancing at it I shut it off and toss it on the counter. The urgent need to scream….to cry….to howl out my pain is fierce and I feel of the ache of holding it all in centered deep in my chest.

Quickly I shed my clothes; the lingering scent of Emma's soft perfume on my shirt speaking once again to my betrayal and deceit. Stepping under the icy spray of the shower, I let the water wash away any remaining telltale signs of what I've done. As it warms, I scrub repeatedly; tearing at my skin with my fingers; hating the person I've let myself become and mumbling over and over, "I'm so sorry Faith. So, so sorry."

+++++++++++++++++++++

When I wake the next morning, I'm completely naked and lying in the middle of the living room floor. I was so out of it last night I barely remember coming in the door, much less anything else that happened. But as I look around, at the pictures scattered around me, I have a fairly good idea that it wasn't pretty.

This has only happened to me a handful times since I lost her. It's like my whole body hits overload and I spiral out of control without realizing it. A few times I've ended up at Grace's; a weeping, slobbery mess and a poor excuse for a man, that's for sure. The other times it's happened, I've managed to handle it on my own. This is the first time, however, that another woman has caused me to completely melt down.

Without question, Emma has stirred up something inside of me that's been dead and dormant for years now. That being said, whatever it is that I think I might feel about her or for her has no place in my life. Not now. Not ever. I'm doing just fine with my meaningless hookups. I sure as hell don't freak out after any of them. All it took was one innocent touch from her and I'm a crazy psycho of regret and need and hurt. I need to shut that shit down. Now.

Pulling myself up, I gather all the pictures and stuff them back into the three boxes that are strewn around the room; shove the entire mess back into the closet. Once I'm dressed in sweats and a t-shirt, I brew a pot of coffee and click the T.V. onto the sports channel.

When the coffee is done and a large mug is in my hand, I locate my phone and turn it on. There are numerous missed calls from Grace and two from Moose. Like me, Ryan is a guy who understands that I just need silence, so I'm not surprised to see that he hasn't tried to contact me.

I delete the calls without listening to the messages; because I already know what they're gonna say. It'll be the same old bullshit….are you okay? Is there anything I can do? What happened? I can't tell them that no, I'm not okay. I'm not ever gonna be okay and there's nothing anyone can do but leave me the hell alone. As far as what happened….well, that's pretty much between me and the ghost of the girl that I love.

Grace has sent a few texts as well and I'm certain she'll show up at my door at some point today. Although, she has gone through her own piles of shit in the past few years, so I get that she understands when you just sometimes need a break from life. I wish I could figure out how to take a permanent break.

I doze off and on all morning and by mid-afternoon I force myself up to do a few chores. My phone has only chimed once a short time ago, and smart girl that she is she didn't even bother to leave a message this time. Grace followed up the call with a text that said simply, *"I'm here."*

I'm busy as all hell at work most of the week, so by the time Friday rolls around I'm grateful for the weekend off that I've been given and plan on spending most of it sleeping. I haven't talked to Grace at all this week, which isn't particularly odd because we both have pretty crazy schedules and sometimes I'll go weeks without seeing or talking to her. Once there was a time when we literally lived in one another's pockets; spending all our time together mourning the loss of our beautiful girl. Somewhere along the line we both realized that we weren't moving forward at all, that whenever we were together it was almost expected that we'd be sad. We each backed off, spending time apart which allowed her time to form her friendship with Moose and to fall in love with Ryan.

Me…well, I managed to drink myself into oblivion and add considerable notches to my bedpost. Clearly, I have some life improvements to work on. I just have no fucking idea how to do that. Not when my heart is still super-glued, locked up and welded to Faith. Not when my head instantly goes to her the minute I feel anything other than lust for another woman.

Not when I might consider that maybe I do want a future; maybe I do want to let the past go.

The thought of letting any part of Faith go makes me physically ill. It feels like the hugest betrayal; like I'm cheating on her or something. She's been so much a part of my life for so long, she is a part of my soul, my entire being. Letting a part of her go would be like cutting off a limb; an unreal choice that would bring with it excruciating pain. It's simply not something I can even consider; and I doubt that I ever will.

Grace appears at my door just as I'm out of the shower; her hands full of pizza and soda. We chat about work while she pulls paper plates out of the cupboard and tells me about this crazy tattoo that Ryan's been working on. Once we're settled on the couch with our food, I wait for the inquisition to begin. I know it's coming, have been expecting it all week, and I have all my token answers ready to go. I'm just that good.

"Have you talked to dad?" she asks, shoving a large bite into her mouth.

I nod. "Yeah. I stopped by a few days ago to take him some cash." Even though my dad has repeatedly told me not to, I'm dead set on repaying him for the fine he covered for me.

"Did he tell you about their cruise?"

I nod and for a few minutes we talk back and forth about dad and Ruth's upcoming trip, Ruth's knee surgery that's scheduled in a few months, and a bunch of other bullshit that has nothing to do with the reason I know she came to hang out with me. By the time we're done eating, we've covered every subject possible; the weather, gas prices, Moose and Autumn's latest break-up and a host of other dumb subjects. And now I'm annoyed and starting to get pissed.

"Why are you really here Grace?"

She frowns, takes our plates and heads into the kitchen. "What do you mean?"

I curse under my breath. "Look, I know you're not here to talk about the weather. So why don't you just come out and say what I know you're dying to say so we can get it the fuck over."

She bustles around in the kitchen, stowing the pizza in the fridge and wiping down the counter. I know she's stalling and I really can't figure out why. Grace has never been one to hold back where I'm concerned.

Getting to my feet, I stomp across the room and rip the dishrag out of her hand. "Say it already!"

Her blue eyes meet mine and she pulls her arms across her chest and leans back against the counter. "You need to let her go Liam."

I expected a lot of things to come out of my sister's mouth; multiple questions asking me what happened between Emma and me, a few inquiries about how I am, and even the inquiry about whether or not I started drinking again. But this? This quiet resolution of facts flowing so effortlessly off her tongue...this I never, ever anticipated.

"Come again?"

"You need to let her go. Faith would not have wanted this for you."

"Would not have wanted what exactly?" I'm pissed off that she's just putting it all out there; pissed off that she's trying to tell me what to do with my life.

Grace throws her hands up. "This! All of this! The drinking, the running away from everything."

"I'm not drinking anymore Grace. I told you that." *Not like I used to anyway.*

She rolls her eyes at me. "I know that. I'm talking about the past few years and this crazy downward spiral that you've been on."

I glare down at her. "Thank you for pointing out how I've fucked up my life."

"Jesus Liam, I'm trying to help!"

I get right down in her face. "I don't want your fucking help!" I expect her to back off, which she will usually do when I get this angry. Instead she pulls herself up and takes a step closer, then shoves at my chest with her small hands.

"Too bad! You're getting it." She stomps across the room, then turns to face me once again. "Look Liam, I understand more than anyone how much you loved Faith. And I envy that, really I do. That kind-of love is beautiful and rare and the fact that you guys had it is amazing. I'll always be grateful to her for how much she loved you." Grace moves closer, her voice shaky and more like a forced whisper. "But she's gone Liam. She's not coming back and all this shit that you're doing to hide from that, to run from it, is only gonna hurt you more." One more step, and she's back in front of me. "I know that whatever happened between you and Emma scared the shit out of you. I'm pretty sure it's the first time you've actually felt anything since you lost Faith."

"Stop it Grace. Just stop it. You need to leave." Her words of truth are like acid on my skin, piercing hot and incredibly agonizing, peeling back the layers of pain one piece at a time.

"It's the truth Liam. You know it is." She starts to reach out and touch me, then immediately pulls her hand back when I flinch in anticipation. "It's okay to feel whatever you're feeling about Emma. You've been alone for almost four years now. It's time to let Faith go."

"No!" I growl. "I'm never gonna let her go."

Tears instantly fill her eyes. "So this is gonna be how you live your life? You're gonna avoid feeling anything for anyone? You're just gonna go around, fucking dumb girls because it feels good?" She swipes at the tears on her face. "Is this what you want for your future? Is this what Faith would have wanted for your future?"

I feel the rage boiling up; the unshed tears that I despise burning in the back of my throat. "You need to leave Grace. Now."

She sniffles a few times and stares up at me with teary blue eyes, like she's trying to pull the truth out from inside my head. When I remain silent and stoic, rigidly standing in front of her and forcing a neutral expression, she finally nods once and turns to retrieve her purse from the coffee table.

I know she knows me well enough not to attempt a hug goodbye, but she does kiss her fingertips and hold them up toward me. "I love you Liam. And Faith loved you too. She would not have wanted any of this for you. She would have hated this person you've become."

Seconds later, she's out the door; leaving me with her words hanging thickly in the air. My reaction is swift and immediate; I slam my fist into the wall, listen as the knuckles crack under the force of my fury. Twice more I pull my arm back, slam it into the drywall, until I'm bleeding and bursts of pain are surging hotly up my arm. Shaking, I slide to the floor and lean against the side of the fridge.

Tears are pouring down my face as I pull my knees to my chest and cover my head with arms. I've felt pain before, felt helplessness before, but this time it's so much more….raw. I'm split in two and bleeding profusely, just as the knuckles on my right hand are. The sobs tear from my chest; shaking my entire body with the force of them and ripping from me the truth…..that I'm as lost as I was the day she left me.

CHAPTER 5

B y the time anniversary number four rolls around, I'm mostly just numb to everything in my life. I haven't spoken to anyone in the past few months, although I will give my sister and friends an A plus for effort. They have tried to reach me; first, it was just a few casual calls from Moose, seeing if I wanted to get together and play pool. Then Grace called to invite me to dinner. And on and on and on.

I ignored each and every call, never returned a text, and refused to answer my door the one and only time Grace attempted to see me. Apparently, with my new found numbness I've also found a new sense of immaturity to go along with it.

Thank God for my job, which keeps me so busy I don't have time to think. With the long fall days and the good weather, we're pounding out job after job and I'm working over seventy hours a week. I have managed to squeeze in a few bed partners here and there, but as before I walk away feeling empty. Only now, I feel empty and guilty; which completely catches me off guard. I have nothing to feel guilty about and not once since Faith's death have any of my fuck buddies caused me an ounce of guilt where she's concerned. Probably because there's no emotion involved, and therefore my exploits are far and removed from anything I once shared with her.

I decide to leave town for the anniversary; partly because I don't want to spend time with my sister and partly because I really need the escape. I know I'm running, like usual, but the thought of seeing the truth in her eyes is something I just don't have the courage to face. I tell no one where I'm going; hop in my truck and just drive toward my destination. I am focused on the task at hand; escape, in any and every way possible.

Las Vegas is the perfect place to disappear; the perfect place for me to hide from everyone who knows me, to hide from all my fears and doubts, to hide from the truth that I wear like a second skin.

I check into a swanky hotel on the strip, take a quick shower and change. The room is nice enough; nice enough for what I've got planned anyway, which isn't pretty. Thirty minutes later I'm out the door, dead-set on my mission to escape in any and every way possible.

When I lift my eyelids the next morning I have this strange feeling of déjà vu. Warm bodies are nestled up against mine on either side; one slim arm is thrown across my chest. Glancing down, I see that the covers are missing and that my two bedmates are wearing high, spiky heels…and nothing else. A black thong is wrapped around my ankle and condom wrappers are scattered over the mattress.

Wow, I think to myself….I have officially hit a new rock bottom.

My head is pounding; a clear reminder that I fell far off the wagon the night before. The little that I do remember are flashes of strobe lights on a dance floor, a girl going down on me in an elevator….quite possibly not one of these girls…..and being thrown out of a club. Or was it two clubs….

Yep….bottom of the barrel, that's for sure.

Slowly, I set aside the arm and slide out from between the two blondes. My head is swimming and my stomach jolts; threatening to surge up if I don't tamp it down. Glancing around, I see that we've done a fairly good job of torching the room. There are more condom wrappers by the large window and what appears to be an impressive dildo on the table in front of the couch. Bottles and glasses litter most of the available surfaces and from what I can gather it's clear that we had a party before the three-way got started. By all the evidence, it's clear that I was seriously on my game last night; either that or there was another guy in attendance. I'm pretty sick knowing that I don't remember if there was or not; nor do I even remember anything about what I did with the blondes. I know only that it was wild and mostly likely out of control.

"Holy fuck," I say to myself.

The need to flee bubbles up like it did the day before and without a second thought I pull on last night's clothes, gather the few items that I have in the bathroom and my cell and head for the door. I'm thankful the girls are still passed out; thankful I can make a clean escape and put this whole nightmare behind me.

Since it's early, and I still have another few days off from work, I quickly gas up the truck, purchase a massive to-go cup of coffee and take off down the highway. I'm heading nowhere fast; running from what I've done, toward the unknown up ahead. *Like I've done for the past four years,* I think as I press down on the gas pedal.

Five hours later I find myself on the road into Grand Canyon National Park. I've been driving on auto-pilot, my hung-over brain barely functioning as I feel a silent pull toward Arizona. I've never been here before; never been anywhere, really. For all the cruises and trips that my dad now takes with Ruth, we never did much as kids other than the occasional overnight campout in the backyard.

The midday sun blasts down through my windshield, and as my headache surges once again I silently remind myself that I should probably get something to eat. As I wind my way through the park, I'm hit with a sudden surge of loneliness; something I haven't felt in months….years maybe. I'm so busy being caught up in just getting by…getting through one day at a time…that I rarely just take a minute to just…exist. Spending all these hours by myself, with no destination in mind, has left me only one clear thought; I'm sick and tired of being alone.

I locate a parking place and take a sweatshirt out of my bag, then head off toward the buildings that are situated on what I'm to assume is the rim of the canyon. I've still not gotten my first look, and like a child on Christmas morning I'm anxious and filled with anticipation. I'm also hit with another strong surge of loneliness; which is immediately followed by a flash of rage. My emotions are all over the board today, which I can only blame on the alcohol and the shit I swam in the night before.

A short time later, I have a sandwich, bottle of water and another of Gatorade in hand and I'm following the crowd toward the rim of the canyon. I walk down the cement path that winds along through trees and cactus and various other plants. It's sunny and cool and the afternoon breeze bites at my face. I eventually come upon an area off to the left of the path; a rocky slope that jets out over the canyon, which is exactly where I plan to park my ass for the rest of the day.

The moment I step up to the edge and gaze out across that breathtaking landscape, there's no question, even to my pessimistic mind, that this place speaks to me on a completely different level than anything I've ever known before. It's majestic, with its layers of different colors, sloping down thousands of feet to the valley below. I can just barely glimpse the Colorado River; the glint from the blue reflection as it snakes along the canyon floor.

In more than four years I've not known one moment's peace. But right here, right now, sitting on the edge of this God-formed creation, I finally feel some of the burden lift that I've been carrying like a dead weight on my shoulders. It's liberating, and at the same time the sadness hits me right in the chest. It's almost like I'm sending part of her away; floating freely on the wind across the miles in front of me.

I sit there for hours, occasionally giving into the tears that feel like they're never going to subside, watching the sun drift overhead and change the color of the canyon walls right before my eyes. The sense of sadness is immense and yet I'm quick to realize that as it slowly fades away with the setting sun, the empty feeling that's been there since I lost her has begun to fade as well.

I end up staying at the park for three more days. I've told no one where I am; called only my boss, who thinks I'm home sick with the flu. Since that call, I've turned my phone off and spent every waking minute walking along the Rim Trail, which traverses along the edge of the Canyon, or wandering through the park itself and just playing tourist. It's a freedom I've never allowed myself to have before and once I'm able to shake off the loneliness I'm able to embrace the sense of calm that takes its place.

I sleep like a log each night; exhausted from the hours of hiking each day and the newfound ability to relax. I spend time sitting in the sun, reading a book about the Canyon history, and pick up some souvenirs to take home to Grace. I know she'll never really understand why I needed to disappear; but I also know that she loves me enough not to question my reasons for needing to.

I feel like a different person as I drive back home at the end of the week, having left the sordid part of myself in Vegas and the broken part in Arizona. I'm no fool; I know this is just the beginning of a very long journey I have to make things right in my head, and in my heart. But it's a good place to start and for the first time in four years I can finally look at myself in the mirror and not cringe.

+++++++++++++++++++++

The first thing I do when I hit the door is shoot Grace a text. I tell her I'm fine, I'm home and ask her to have dinner with me over the weekend. I have a lot that I need to make right with my sister, especially since we haven't talked at all since the night we fought. Now that my fog has cleared, I'm finally able to see that she only said those things because she loves me. She truly and completely believes it's time for me to let go and move on. I might not be able to do that yet, but the baby steps I've taken this past week are a good start.

Once I've started some laundry, I tear through the apartment like a crazy man; cleaning every surface, vacuuming the carpets and thoroughly disinfecting the bathroom. The kitchen is a cesspool of bad food and spilled stains, but after working diligently for over an hour it finally sparkles and looks presentable. By the time laundry load number two is folded and put away, I'm exhausted and fall into bed; asleep before my head hits the pillow.

The next morning I'm awakened by pounding on the front door; a furious thump I recognize all too well as my sister's. Dragging on sweats, I click the locks open and greet her with a smile; which I can instantly tell catches her off-guard.

"Hey big brother, how the hell are you?"

I step back to let her in and move into the kitchen to get the coffee going. "Pretty good. And you?"

She's glancing around my place, a frown deeply imbedded between her eyes. "Um Liam, is there someone living with you now?"

"No. Why?"

"Cuz your place is spotless."

I chuckle. "Yeah, I cleaned."

"Wow."

"Yeah, it was pretty bad." I cringe inwardly, thinking about the piles of garbage and filth that I took out to the trash; the layers upon layers of grime that I washed away….four years of neglect gone in just a few hours.

Grace settles on the couch, one slim leg over the other. "So, where have you been?"

I flop down onto the opposite end and run my fingers through my messy hair. "Um…well I was out of town."

She nods. "Okay. Is everything all right? Where did you go?"

I debate whether or not to be honest with her, until the voice in my head reminds me that I've never been anything but. "Well, I started off in Vegas."

"Oh fuck," she says.

Wrinkling up my nose, I reply, "You have no idea."

She folds her arms across her chest. "Let me guess, it involved booze and girls."

I nod. "Yep. A lot of both."

"Jesus Liam."

"I know sis. Believe me, I know." I've yet to get the images out of my head; my downward spiral into hell ending in a swanky hotel room where I said fuck you to everything.

"So, have you been there all this time?"

"No. Just one night was enough. I took off the next morning and headed toward Arizona. I've been at the Grand Canyon for most of the week." I see the look of shock cross her face, followed immediately by concern.

"Are you okay?"

I consider her question. Am I okay? Yeah, I guess I am. Am I sad? Yeah. Am I lonely? Hell yeah. Am I relieved that I was able to let some shit go? Absolutely. "Yeah Gracie, I think I am okay."

She smiles at me. "How about us? Are we okay?"

I reach for her hands. "We are definitely okay."

Tears fill her eyes. "I've been so worried about you Liam. You've been so…unreachable."

"I know. And I'm sorry. I think I just needed to finally hit rock bottom. Now that I have, I guess I can start figuring shit out again." I realize as I say the words that this isn't the first time I've admitted to myself that I've hit rock bottom, and I gotta wonder….have I really gone as low as I can go, or is there more bad stuff on the horizon?

She swipes at her face, then immediately threads her fingers with mine again. "Did you hit rock bottom in Vegas?"

I cringe. "Oh yeah. As low as I could have ever been, that's for sure." My eyes find hers. "I don't remember much of what happened that night. I woke up in a room filled with condom wrappers, two strangers in my bed and a massive hangover."

"God, you are such a fucking whore," she remarks with a shiver.

I laugh. "Yeah, that's a true statement." I head into the kitchen and get our coffee; hand a steamy cup to her and sip from my own.

"So, tell me about the Grand Canyon."

I have no idea how to put into words all that I found while I was there; and all that I was able to let go of. I feel lighter now, less burdened by my life, by the sadness that's surrounded me for so long. "I don't know how to explain it Grace, but being there…." I search for just the right words. "Being there changed me."

Her head cocks to the side. "You do seem different. More like the old Liam."

I shrug. "Yeah, I can't tell you why, but something about that place….." I shake my head, unable to find the right words to explain my thoughts.

"I'm glad. I hope you were able to let some of the stuff that hangs on you go."

"I was. I let a lot of stuff go out there. A lot of stuff that needed to be let go years ago."

She nods in understanding and I know in my heart that she really, truly does understand. Only Grace has ever known the enormity of the pain that I live with; because she lives with the exact same thing. She's managed to figure out how to live with the pain; give it its place and time, but not let it encompass her entire life anymore. Now it's my turn to learn how to do the same.

We end up spending the entire day together; a long overdue day of doing nothing but enjoying one another's company. I take her to breakfast at our favorite hole-in-the-wall, then we swing by her place and pick up a few some things and head out to the beach. We stay there for most of the day, then meet up with Ryan and Moose for burgers. It's a relaxed, fun evening; one I haven't had since I can't remember when. And for once, I actually have some hope that my future won't consist of long, sleepless nights and never-ending heartache. For once, I actually have hope that I'll be happy; that I may actually have a bright future. I've got a lot to be grateful for. I've got a great job, a decent place to live, an amazing family and great friends. I really need to start being grateful for what I do have, and stop spending so much time whining about what I don't have. It's a work in progress; I'm sure as hell a work in progress, but for once I don't dread the idea of tomorrow. For once I'm actually curious and hopeful about my future.

CHAPTER 6

Thanksgiving and Christmas fly by; a flurry of too much work and very little time left for relaxation. We're trying to cram in every job we can before the rainy season sets in; which for California is always less than impressive. That being said, we're forecasted to have an El Nino year, and to those of us that live here that equals a decent amount of rain for a change.

Grace invites me to the annual New Year's Eve bash at our favorite bar, and even though I'm hesitant to be around all the partiers, I do now have full control of myself and complete management where alcohol is concerned, or at least that's the line of bull I keep repeating again and again in my head. Vegas pretty much cured me of any need to ever get hammered again. For the foreseeable future, at least.

I head to the bar around ten, after I swing by and pick up Moose. He's now off-again with Autumn, and in full Moose mode; ready to tie one on and hopefully take home a willing lady. Reminds me of the old me.

We shoot the shit while we drive and as usual he keeps me laughing. I'm grateful, as always, for his easy friendship. He never has a need to push me for anything deep, but the unspoken support is always right there at the surface. I can easily see why he's fast becoming my best friend too.

The place is packed to the gills when we arrive, but somehow Moose manages to surge his mammoth body forward and get us a spot at the bar. He orders beers; my one and only and his first of many. We clink the bottles together and once again he launches off into one of his stories. We take bets with one another on who here tonight will be still be standing at midnight, who will need to be carried out, and which one of the four gals he has his eyes on he'll end up taking home. He may be a big guy, but the ladies flock to him.

44

Grace and Ryan finally make an appearance and by the flush on my sister's cheeks I'm guessing they started their celebration in the car; and it didn't involve clothes. We share hugs all around, and after she gives me the stink-eye about my beer, they take off toward the dance floor. It's then that I see a familiar dark haired beauty heading my way; apprehension and uncertainty written in the amazing eyes she turns in my direction.

"Hi Liam," she replies.

"Hey Emma. How are you?" I get to my feet and gesture for her to take my bar stool.

"I'm good. And you?"

I give Moose a head nod and he discretely takes off; leaving me free to assume his seat. "I'm pretty good thanks. What can I get you?"

"I'll have what you're having," she says.

I order a beer and glance over at her; take in the massive cascade of thick dark hair and force the image of it draped across my chest from my head. "How's the café?"

She smiles up at me. "So good. The holidays were crazy, but business was steady and the customers were happy, so that's all that matters."

I grin down at her. "That's really great."

"Grace ended up being a huge help. Didn't she tell you?"

I shake my head and stare down into my bottle. "No she didn't." I don't tell her it's because I assume my sister is very careful never to mention her name.

Emma frowns. "Oh. Well, anyway, yeah, she's been working with me most nights and sometimes on the weekends." She leans over, like she's gonna tell me a state secret. "I'm trying to get her to come work with me permanently."

This is news to me. I always thought Grace loved her job working for a cell phone company. And yeah, in the past few years she's become an amazingly self-taught chef, but doing it full time seems a little risky. "What does she say about that?"

She takes a sip from her bottle and shrugs. "She's unsure, mostly about the money, which I understand."

"Yeah."

We sit there together, surrounded by loud people, even louder music, and yet it feels like it's just she and I; this awkwardly forced together duo that spend a helluva lot of time ignoring the obvious. I can tell by her mannerisms, the hesitation I still see in her eyes, that she's unsure what my reaction will be to her; especially since I imploded right in front of her the last time we were together.

"So…" I begin, after what feels like at least fifteen minutes of silence, "I owe you an apology."

She frowns. "You do? Why?"

I rub my forehead and stare into the mirror that's located behind the bar. "For acting like an ass that night and walking away when we were playing pool."

"It's really okay Liam. I understand."

I glance over at her, see her biting her lower lip; feel the tug of her teeth center right in my gut. "You do?"

She nods. "Well, yeah. Obviously something upset you that night and you needed to leave."

Perplexed by her easy-going attitude, I push on. "So, Grace didn't tell you anything or try to explain?"

She shrugs. "Not really. I asked if you were okay, she said no. When I asked why she said it was a long story. It wasn't really my place to want to know more."

"Do you? Want to know more, I mean?" I have no idea where this is all coming from. It's almost like my mouth is five steps in front of my head.

"Only if you want me to."

I'm floored. This breathtaking, amazing woman is not pushing me for an explanation or bitching about how I treated her. She's open and willing to listen, which is so much more than I could ever ask for; so much more than I deserve.

Leaning my chin on my fist, I glance over and state, "I lost someone…. someone I loved." I'm still not used to saying it in the past tense and I feel the pain of the words hit me right between the eyes.

"I'm so sorry," she whispers, the sound barely audible over the noise in the bar.

I nod. "Me too." Draining my beer, I resist the urge to request another; choose instead to face the demons that are threatening head on. "Anyway, I just hadn't been….close…with anyone since her."

Emma raises her eyebrow at me. "Really?"

"Well, I've been with people, but not close. Not like we were that night." *Not so close that I felt it deep in my pores…and like I never wanted to let you go.*

Her cheeks flame and she averts her eyes. "Oh. Okay."

"I was pretty freaked out. And I acted like a tool, just leaving like that. I'm really sorry." I reach for her hand, disengage it from the bottle that she has a firm grip on, and weave our fingers together. Like that night months ago, I feel her touch engulf me fully and rip the breath clear out of my throat.

"So is that why you haven't come by the café?"

I nod. "Yeah, I guess so. I needed to work out a lot of shit."

"And did you?"

I smile over at her. "It's a work in progress."

"So does that mean you'll dance with me?" Her large brown eyes are sparkling up at me and damn if she isn't biting on her lip again.

Getting to my feet, I reply, "Yes, I'll dance with you." She's smiling as I lead her toward the back of the room, where couples are entwined around one another even though the song is fairly upbeat. I pull her close, release her hand from mine so that I can skim my fingertips around her waist. She wraps her arms around my neck, nestles her silky head just under my chin and we start to move together slowly.

This time when I touch her there's no fear, no anticipation, no emptiness that's immediately followed by images of Faith. This time it's just the two of us, two strangers working on a friendship. I'd like to think that we might eventually be more, but my ability to hope for that is tainted by my past; by the pain and fear that still lingers. For now, I'm content to simply enjoy her company; just enjoy the feel of a woman in my arms.

"You okay?" she whispers, tipping her head back to look up at me.

I nod and smile down at her. "Yeah Em, I'm good." As her head settles back against my chest, my eyes meet Grace's from across the room. She smiles, though I still see a trace of sadness there; the hint that like me, she's beginning to see Faith's hold on us lessening a little bit, each and every day. It's a terrifying thought, and one I find myself fighting against day after day. But then I experience this….this crazy whole-body reaction to just sharing a simple dance with Emma, and I know I'm finally on the right path.

We stay on the dance floor swaying together silently while the room moves on around us. Occasionally, Grace and Ryan will enter my line of vision…or Moose, with his bevy of arm candy draped around his body. But mostly it's just the two of us; content to just enjoy the evening together.

By the time the countdown for New Year's is on, I'm starting an internal debate about how to handle it. I don't want to lead her on; but I also don't want to give her the impression that I'm not interested. Obviously, I am. But the fine line between what I want and what's best for me is clearly something that I need to work on - among other things - and certainly something that is not going to be defined tonight.

The room erupts around us; shouts of 'Happy New Year's', lots of hugging and kissing and more than one bottle being tapped with another. I glance down, see the wide smile Emma sends my way; watch her lips move in what I'm going to assume is her well wish for the New Year. Since I can't hear her, I mouth the same back and assume she'll understand.

Then she throws me off guard; rises up on her tip toes until we are almost face to face, and pulls my head towards hers. The kiss is brief, feather light, and like her touch I feel it everywhere; racing through my blood and warming me from the inside out. It's been years since I shared a simple kiss. Those I've experienced the past few years have been mostly hunger fueled and the gateway to the fuck-fest after. This is sweet and simple and before I know it, it's over.

Part of me wants to pull her close and kiss her again; deep and hard and thoroughly like my body is pushing me to. But the hesitant part of me, the part of me that is still unsure and oddly terrified of getting close to this amazing woman, rules my head. I set her back slightly, just enough to gather her hand in mine once again, and go in search of our friends.

We find them at our usual spot, back by the pool tables. I leave Emma's side long enough to hug my sister and the guys, wish them Happy New Year's, then after she does the same we link hands once again. It all feels so damn normal, and so incredibly easy; like putting one foot in front of the other of opening your eyes in the morning. Normal….natural…easy.

"Dude, I gotta find me a chick to take home," Moose says, draining his shot and slamming the glass down. "I'm horny as hell." We laugh, Grace slaps him in the center of his massive chest and I watch as Emma's face grows redder by the minute. Moose, dog that he is, acts shocked at our outbursts and states loudly, "What? I need to get laid. Sue me for crying out loud."

I glance over at Emma and can tell by the look on her face that she wants to disappear into the floor. Turning to give my buddy a dirty look, I growl, "Hey man, tone it down."

Moose looks at Emma, and quickly realizes she's not schooled in his usual talk. "Ah fuck, I'm sorry darlin'."

She laughs. "It's okay Moose. At least you're saying exactly what's on your mind."

He laughs and points at me. "Ha! Right?"

We stand around and talk for a while; the place is too packed tonight to even think about playing pool. Moose takes off, his eyes on a hot blonde across the room; one I'm positive I screwed a few months ago. It's a sobering thought and the very excuse I need to be on my way.

"I'm gonna take off."

"Me too," Emma replies. "Walk me out?"

My stomach jumps around nervously, but I manage to reply, "Of course."

We say our goodbyes and once again Grace gives me the stink-eye; this time I'm certain it's more of a warning to keep it in my pants than a look of irritation that I got earlier. I take Emma's hand and we weave our way through the mass of people and out through the front door. People are gathered in the front of the building; laughing, smoking and generally having a good time. We move past them out into the parking lot, where she points to a small blue compact car.

By the time we're at her car I'm almost shaking with anxiety; something I haven't felt to this extreme since way back…years ago…the first time I kissed Faith. That was a lifetime ago, but the insecurity and fear remain; and now I have the lingering guilt which lays over me like a thick fog.

"Thanks for tonight Liam. It was a lot of fun." Our hands are still linked and she fishes in her pocket for her keys with her free one. "Hope to see you at the café soon."

I nod. "Yeah. I'd like that. I miss those tortilla things."

She rolls her eyes at me and starts to laugh. "Cannoli."

I laugh down at her. "Oh yeah. Cannoli. Got it."

Her eyes roll again. "Yeah, I doubt it."

We spend a few long moments staring at one another, then she slowly pulls her fingers from mine until we are fully separated and I can take a step back. The foreign feeling of regret races through me and I'm not sure what to make of it, so I shove it aside and attempt to ignore it.

"Take care of yourself," she replies, then pulls open the car door and slides behind the wheel.

"You too."

As I watch her drive away I'm bombarded with emotions; so much so that I'm having a hard time breathing…again. I've gotten so used to feeling empty, feeling nothing, that all of these things at once are scaring me to death. I'm sweating and shaking and the familiar urge to run is back once again.

I'm not running this time. I may want to…and yeah, I may need to, but I'm staying here and facing this shit once and for all. Emma scares me; that's a fact. But those feelings of fear are not gonna go away if I avoid her. They may get worse if I spend more time with her, but as long as I'm very careful to maintain a good distance between us, and just concentrate on our friendship, I should be okay.

++++++++++++++++++++++

The following Saturday I resume my weekly café stops. I give myself plenty of extra time, just in case Emma and I decide to have a real conversation instead of the ones we used to have which lasted all of ten seconds.

The minute I walk through the café door the feeling of coming home hits me like a freight train. Familiar scents, the opera music, her laughter from the back room, all fill me with a sense of calm I didn't realize that I'd been missing.

"Be right with you," her voice rings out.

The pastry case is filled to overflowing and I'm happy to see a good supply of cannoli just calling to me from their spot on the bottom shelf. My mouth is watering in anticipation and by the time she makes an appearance I'm like a drug addict; needing my fix in the worst way.

"Hey!" she replies. "Good to see you."

I grin at her. "You too Em. But I'm a desperate man in need of at least a dozen of those tortilla things. Stat."

She glares at me. "Liam Mathers, if you don't call them by their correct name you're getting nothing."

I chuckle under my breath. "Cana…canacoli….canolopoly…."

She mutters a curse and rolls her eyes. "C..a..n..n..o..l..i." She says the word slowly, like I'm a five year old or completely inept. I'm quite positive there are a handful of times during the past four years that I've been a whole shit-ton of both.

I can't help but laugh at her. "Yeah, I know. I like pissing you off and calling them by the wrong name."

Emma shakes her dark head at me and pulls a plate and a fork from behind the counter. No paper bag for me this time, I notice. I wish women weren't so confusing and I knew what to make of this change. "You're ridiculous." She plops two pastries down on the plate and hands them over. "Sit. I'll bring your coffee."

"Yes ma'am," I reply, liking this side of her.

I'm already half-way through one when she takes the seat across from me; sets two cups of coffee down on the table and sends me a shit-eating grin. "You are so addicted to those."

I moan, then finish the bite in my mouth before saying, "You have no idea. I could seriously eat twenty of them without thinking twice."

She swipes one finger through the filling that has plopped out onto my plate; sucks the sweetness onto her pink tongue. I feel that gesture right in my gut, then lower, and the need to adjust myself is blurring my vision.

"You working today?" she asks, sipping at her coffee and continuing to molest the leftover filling on the plate.

I nod, because actually speaking right now will be a challenge. I force my eyes off her mouth and anywhere else but the tempting pink warmth that screams silent promises to me.

"Grace is here. She's is the kitchen making cookies."

"Really?" I manage, though it comes out sounding strained and a little too high. Her knowing smirk and wide grin tell me she knows exactly what she's doing. When she reaches out again, I grip her wrist, growling, "Please stop." What I really want is to watch her lick that filling off me, or rather, off certain parts of me.

She starts to laugh, crosses one leg over the other and sits back in her chair, cup in hand. "Sorry."

I press the heels of my hands to my eyes. "Yeah, okay."

Thankfully, my sister decides to make an appearance; which effectively halts our strange conversation and puts an end to the uncomfortable situation between my legs.

"Hey big brother!" she hugs me quickly, sending flour all over my shirt. She glances down at my plate. "Ah, see you can't resist Emma's cannoli."

Emma giggles and I throw her a look. "Um yeah, they are awesome."

Grace is oblivious and spends a few minutes telling me all about the crap she's baking back there, but all I can do is stare at Emma; at her eyes, at that damn tempting mouth of hers, until I swear I'm seeing cross-eyed and I'm starting to sweat.

"Well, gotta run. See ya." Grace smacks my cheek with a kiss and trots back into the kitchen, leaving the two of us still staring at one another. The spell isn't broken until the bell over the door peels, and we're both left blinking repeatedly.

"I'll box this up for you and get you a to-go cup," she says, hurriedly getting to her feet. I watch in silence as she greets the customer and gets my items ready; gives me a little head nod gesture to retrieve them from the counter. When I start to pull out my wallet, she frowns and shakes her head, then turns her attention back to the customer. I drop the cash in the tip jar and head for the door without looking back.

+++++++++++++++++++++

Emma

For months now I've wondered what it is that I did to drive Liam away that night we were playing pool. One minute, we were horsing around, trying to pull a fast one on our friends, and the next he's turning to stone right before my eyes; not to be seen again for many long months. I did ask Grace about it, but her reaction was so much like his that I let it go; just chalked it up to yet another relationship ending before it really got started.

I really like Liam. I like the way he talks to me, the gentle way he touches me; and even the occasional fire that I see in his eyes when he thinks I don't notice. Celebrating New Year's together was amazing, and getting to know him, having him apologize to me, was what I've wanted and hoped for… for months now.

I know he's a tortured guy and I have my suspicions that it has something to do with Faith, the friend that comes up in conversations sometimes when I'm with Grace and Ryan. I've seen her pictures in Grace's apartment and the tattoo that she has on her wrist and I'm sure there's a boatload of history there that I don't dare ask about. Grace will tell me when she's ready, and so will he.

I was quite stunned when he did apologize and did attempt to explain his reaction to me. I know it was hard for him; I could see the pain in his eyes, the agony that he and Grace both wear like a second skin. I'm so afraid of saying the wrong thing or doing the wrong thing; and yet when I'm with him I just seem to react and not think at all.

Like when we were dancing and I kissed him. I'm no dummy; I know the guy would eagerly get into my panties if I said or did a few more obvious things. I'm also fairly certain I'd eagerly hand myself over to him; he's darn tempting with those dreamy blue eyes and that rock hard body.

That being said, I know I gotta stop flirting with him. It's clear to me that whatever this is between us, we are starting with a friendship. All that business with the cannoli, while I clearly enjoyed seeing him squirm, was very unnecessary. If he is as tortured as I think he is, he needs honesty, friendship and someone who will be nothing but straight with him. There's no place for flirting or head games or any of that crap with this guy.

"Hey lady," Grace calls from the kitchen. "You gonna help me back here or stay out there daydreaming all day?"

I chuckle, pull myself upright and head into the kitchen. We are locked up for the day and once again she's here; my savior, my (hopefully) soon to be partner, my very dear friend. We work together finishing the last few batches of dough, and then I start the water running and dive into the pile of dishes.

Thirty minutes later we're seated at a small table in the front, glasses of wine and a plate of cheese and crackers between us. Grace finishes her conversation with Moose and stows the phone in her back pocket. Then her eyes are on me while her fingertips tap against the glass. "So, what's going on with you and my brother?"

I half-way expected this; especially since Liam and I were so cozy at the bar the week before. "Um, I'm not sure. We're friends."

Grace rolls her eyes. "Friends my ass. You two were ready to strip naked and go for it this morning."

My face flames and I take a big slurp of the merlot; let it ease the tension in my body. "Um, well, that sorta got out of hand."

She raises one dark brow at me. "You think?"

I steeple my hands and look across at her. "He apologized to me, for how he behaved that night we were playing pool. And he tried to explain to me why he acted that way."

Grace nibbles on a cracker. "What did he say?"

I shrug. "Not much. Only that he loved someone and lost her. And that it's been a long time since he's been close with someone."

Grace frowns. "Hmm. Interesting."

"Why do you say that?"

She shrugs. "Well, my brother is a little...shall we say....loose with his morals."

I'm not the least bit surprised. A guy that looks like he does probably has to fend women off daily. "Yeah, I understand that. He meant that he hadn't been close like that. Like we were." I watch her intently; see that same haunted expression cross her face, the same one that Liam wears most of the time. "Grace, what's going on?"

Grace sits back in her chair and shakes her head. "It's not my place to talk about it Em. You should ask Liam."

I nod, feel the hope leave my body completely. "Can you tell me this? Do you believe he's ever gonna be ready for anything other than friendship or is he only interested in a...quickie?"

Grace chuckles, but it's short lived. "I don't know. I hope he's ready for more than a quickie. He's a pretty tough nut to crack. I do worry about him though, all the time."

"Yeah, okay." It's not okay, but I don't tell her that. I also don't tell her that I'm falling fast and hard for her brother; a man I'm sure is untouchable.

She reaches out and takes my hand. "Just give him some time. If you really like him, just be patient and give him time to sort this all out in his head."

"Okay."

I've always been a fairly impatient person, so I know this will really be a test of the true me. If I can stick this out, stick by him and let him see that I'm in it for the long haul, then maybe, just maybe he'll start to meet me half way. I just hope that my need to want to help him doesn't outweigh the need I know he has to let me in a little at a time.

Grace grins across at me. "You totally have the hots for him, don't you?"

I slump against my hands, cup my chin and look at her. "Yes, I do. He's just so....yummy."

Grace starts to cackle...loudly...and all I can do is hide my red face in my arms on the table. "Yummy? Did you seriously just say that about my brother?"

I lift my head just enough to glare at her. "I hate you, you know that, right?"

She starts to laugh again. "Yummy! What a hoot!"

I shake my head, tip up my glass and drain it completely; even though I'm well aware that no amount of good red wine will cure this ache. Yeah, he may be yummy and I most definitely wouldn't complain if I saw him naked, but thinking about the months….or years….that I may spend alone if he eventually changes his mind about me, is a little frightening. I've been alone a long time; too long actually for someone my age. I've been so driven by my work, my life that's tied up in this café, that life around me has just slipped right on by.

I'm not letting it slip by any more.

CHAPTER 7

Saturday mornings at the café start to become what I plan my week around; and on the odd chance that I'm not working, I go anyway. The first Saturday following the cannoli eating incident things were pretty damn awkward between us. Emma kept averting her eyes and I know that I didn't make things any easier by immediately telling her that I was in a hurry. I wasn't, but I needed her to know that I didn't have time to corner her about what happened, and I sure as hell didn't have time for a repeat performance.

The following week things are better between us. The weird tension has subsided and there's almost a sense of acceptance drifting from her to me. The café is oddly packed, probably because I'm late heading to the site. She doesn't have time to talk, but piles a bag high with cannoli and some other things I can't pronounce, and shoots me a wink across the counter.

Yep....I feel that where I shouldn't.

By week number three the days are crawling and by Wednesday I'm out of work for a few days because of the non-stop rain we've had. I say to hell with my normal plan of doing a whole lot of nothing and climb in my truck and head over to the café. There's no way in hell I'm waiting until Saturday to see her.

Her happy look of surprise warms me in all the right places; and in a few not so good places either, I admit. I wait my turn behind the two customers in front of me, and use my time to simultaneously check her out and peruse the pastry case. By the time I step up to the counter and grin at her, she holds up one finger and shakes it at me; obviously catching me in the act of looking at her ass yet again.

"This is a nice surprise," she grins.

"I'm not working today, so I thought I'd see if you saved me any of those tortilla things."

She shakes her head at me and forces a frown. "That, sir, will get you dish duty."

I shrug. "Put me to work. I have nothing to do today."

Emma frowns at me. "Are you serious?"

"Hell yeah. Especially if I can have all the tortilla things I want."

She shakes her head at me again and leans down under the counter, takes out an apron and throws it at my chest. "All right big guy, come on. I've got a list of things you can help me with."

"Promises, promises."

She turns and tosses me what is supposed to be a stern look, then starts to laugh because she just can't hold it together any longer. I follow her into the small kitchen area, where the counters are stacked with bowls, trays of pastries just out of the oven and numerous other things that I can't even begin to name. It all looks to me like an over-abundance of chaos and too damn much work, and I seriously cannot believe that this tiny woman can do it all by herself.

"Christ Em, how do you keep up with all this?"

She shrugs nonchalantly. "I just…do, I guess. Grace has been amazing and I couldn't have gotten through the holiday season without her."

I quickly tie the apron around my waist. "Okay boss, where do you want me." I watch as her eyes do a quick stroll up and down my body and I'm positive she's not thinking about dish washing. "Uh Em, eyes right here." I point to my face.

Her cheeks blaze bright red. "Shut up." She heads over to the sink and gives me the standard 'come here' gesture with her index finger. I listen intently as she starts to give me orders, although I gotta admit that it's completely hot having a chick tell me what to do and I spend more time fantasizing about her than actually paying attention to what she's saying. I like the way she tells me what to do and I gotta wonder if she does that in bed too.

"You good?"

"I'm so g…." I stop myself, rein back the naughty talk. "Yep. I can handle this."

She grins. "Okay. Holler if you need something."

I spend the entire day washing every dish, all the pans and numerous other items that she drops on the counter near me. Granted, I do have an industrial dishwasher to handle the bulk of the items, but the large stuff I do by hand. She darts back and forth, handling the customers and the front counter, and when it's slow starting the recipes for the next day. It's a brutal merry-go-round of constant work, with the enticing smells and soft opera music to help lighten the load.

In the early afternoon she makes us sandwiches on fresh homemade bread and I seriously have to force myself not to moan it's so damn good. We eat together sitting on stools behind the counter, and she keeps up a running dissertation about things she still needs to improve on and items she wants to add to the case.

She's vivacious and animated as she talks, waving her hands around and talking a mile a minute; barely pausing long enough to take a bite. She tells me all about her Nana, who taught her how to cook, and how's she dreamed of having a café like this since she was a child. I'm completely enamored by her - by the sound of her voice, the soft chime of her laughter – and I'm well aware of the fact that I'm mostly in over my head where she's concerned.

By closing time, I take over the clean-up duties out front while she gets back to work on the pastries. Once I've mopped the floors, wiped down the tables and closed the front blinds, I head back into the kitchen where Emma is at the long, oak work table, rolling out dough with her small hands. This simple act is intoxicating and just one more thing that I feel over my entire body.

Shoving the need aside, I park the cleaning supplies in the small room at the back, then move back into the kitchen and ask, "Anything else I can do?"

She smiles at me. "No thanks. I can't tell you how much I appreciate you being here today."

I walk up next to her. "I'm off again tomorrow, so I'll be here bright and early." The idea of spending another day with her makes me really too happy.

Her hands stop the kneading motion and she looks up at me. "Don't you have stuff you need to do?"

Shaking my head, I reply, "No. Obviously there's plenty to be done here."

She laughs. "That's an understatement."

Our eyes meet and hold and for that moment I'm certain that I don't remember to breathe. Being around her today and just going about the duties at hand has given me quite the insight to this woman I am intrigued by. She's an extremely hard worker and singularly driven to see her business, her life's dream, be successful. But it's her sweet disposition, the quick humor, and the flash of need that I see in her eyes….like I do right now….that reassure my head that I'm moving in the right direction.

Even if my heart doesn't quite believe it yet.

She blinks twice and takes a shaky breath, then immediately resumes her task with the dough. I never once believed that seeing someone doing such a simple task could be such a turn on; but the strength in her small hands, the gentle way she pushes and pulls the dough just how she wants it, quite literally leaves me heated up and breathing way too fast.

Without thinking I move behind her; wrap my arms around her waist and pull her against my body. I hear her quick intake of breath, watch as her hands still on the dough. "Don't stop. Keep going." She slowly starts again, while at the same time I bury my face in her hair; breathe in the soft flowery scent and press a kiss to the top of her head. She tips her head to the side, granting me access to the long slope of her neck. When my lips touch her skin, I hear a soft sigh escape her lips and her hands start to slow once again.

"Keep going Em," I whisper.

My hands slide up her waist, up to her shoulders and down the length of her arms. Back and forth I drag my fingertips; down to her hands and back up to her shoulders. She immediately reacts to my touch; goosebumps lighting her silky skin with each trail of my fingers. I do this twice more before I settle my hands at her waist and pull her snug against me once more.

"Liam?" she says softly, eyes closed as I continue to travel my lips down her neck.

"Yeah."

She's silent, yet I can hear the debate in her head as if she said the words out loud. I know this, because it's the same argument I'm having with myself; one that's getting louder and more annoying with each passing minute. It would be so easy to strip off our clothes and put an end to all this tip-toeing around one another. It would be so easy to go to that place I'm so used to going. It would be so easy to end us before we even started.

Standing upright, I drop one more kiss on her head and take two steps back. Our mutual sighs of relief, regret even, fill the kitchen as I move slowly out of the room. "See you tomorrow."

"Okay. Thanks again."

As I drive home I find that I'm very conflicted. It's obvious that she wants me just as much as I want her. It's also obvious to me that she's hesitant to get involved with me. Now whether or not that's because of the baggage that I wear like clothing or just the vibe she picks up from me, I don't know. What I do know is that I need to spend however much time I have with her, getting to know her and letting her know me.

A white hot slice of betrayal shoots through my heart and instantly Faith's face flashes in my mind. I thought I'd moved past that; thought I'd made progress in my ability to give Faith her place in my life, without dragging down any future I might have. Clearly, there are unresolved issues where she's concerned and once again I'm thankful I put a stop to what Emma and I were doing.

I wonder if it will always be like this; one step forward, twenty steps back. There are times I feel so free from the burden I carry; like today when I was working at the café and just hanging out with Emma. For the first time in forever I actually felt like a normal, regular guy. Then there are times, more times than I can count actually, when memories and thoughts and feelings seem to hit me out of left field. Suddenly I'm right back where I was a year ago, and a year before that, consumed by my lost love and unable to imagine a future without her.

++++++++++++++++++++

I spend the next two days working alongside Emma. My being there gives her the freedom to do what she does best; taking care of the customers and taking the time to visit with each one. My being there gives me the freedom to relax around her and hopefully settle into this friendship without the fears that seem to forever be waiting on the doorstep of my heart.

Working together side by side gives me ample opportunities to learn things about her. She tells me all about her Italian grandparents, who emigrated from Italy when they both were youngsters. She tells me some stories from her childhood, talks about her brother Mario and gushes about her parents.

"What's your last name?" I inquire while we're eating lunch one afternoon.

"Matticelli."

I laugh. "Christ. Doesn't get any more Italian than that."

"I know, right?"

I'm fully aware that she keeps her questions for me about the normal stuff; stories from our childhood, stuff about my dad and Grace. Only once does she probe too close when she asks about my mom; the woman who walked away without a backwards glance to the two kids she was leaving behind. Whatever Emma sees on my face must convince her that this is a subject I'm not comfortable talking about, because she immediately changes the subject.

I notice that she's very careful to never ask about previous relationships that I might have had. Of course, I don't go there either. I guess there are just some things I don't need to know; some things I don't want to know.

Grace appears Friday afternoon and after giving me the third degree about why I'm there she settles in and starts baking. As I put away the clean dishes, I marvel at my crazy sister who a few years ago couldn't boil water. Now she's perfecting the art of Italian pastry.

By seven that evening we're all exhausted, starving and in need of a good meal and a cocktail. Ryan joins us when he's done for the night and the four of us head out to a local Mexican joint down the street. We eat two baskets of chips before the meal and even though Grace is still giving me the stink-eye I reward my hard kitchen duty with my one beer of the evening.

Emma and I sit together in the booth and I'm amazed at how easily we slide into togetherness; trying bites off each other's plates, her reaching for my hand under the table. It's a good feeling, being normal again, out on this pseudo double date. I haven't dated...really dated....in so many years I can't even remember what it was like. I mostly avoided that scene, until Faith came along. And then we were too busy being naked to care about going out to dinner or seeing a movie.

The familiar feeling of betrayal slowly eases into my head; my heart. I try shoving it back, ignoring it, giving it its due then setting it aside. But nothing works. Every time I look at Emma I think about Faith and how I'm betraying her. Every time I feel Emma's fingers against mine, my entire body reacts with tension.

"You okay?" she whispers.

I nod, pull my hand out of hers and drag it through my hair. "Yeah. Food didn't settle well I guess." I risk a look at Grace; see the concern etched in her eyes. "I should probably head home."

"I'll go too," Emma replies.

Shaking my head, I get to my feet and throw some cash at Ryan. "No, that's okay. You stay. I'll see you tomorrow." I'm out the door before anyone can pull me back; my memories once again chasing me onward. Sadly, I can't even let myself feel regret about leaving Emma high and dry like that; I'm so submersed in anything and everything Faith.

That night I toss and turn and the snippet of time that I do sleep I'm tormented by images of her; bald and screaming out in pain, begging me to take it away, take her away. By two I'm wide awake, sitting on my couch with my phone in my hand, dialing Grace's number.

"Liam?" she says without greeting, answering on the first ring. "Are you okay?"

"Can I get Emma's number from you?" In my head I know that I'm going to call her in the morning; make up some dumb excuse not to go into the café. I remind myself that I could just as easily call the café directly and not be bothered with trying to reach her on her cell.

"Sure, of course." She rattles off the number, which I promptly scribble down, then, "Are you sure you're okay? I can come over."

"I'm fine Grace. Sorry I bothered you."

"It's fine. Love you big brother."

"Love you too."

I sit there for a half hour, staring at her number and telling myself that I shouldn't call her; I can't call her. Dumping my shit on her will solve nothing; it sure as hell won't bring us closer, not that I'm even sure at this point if that's what I want. What I want is for my life to move forward. And every step I take it seems like I keep getting pulled back into that dark abyss by the chains of Faith's memory.

I dial the numbers quickly and before I can hang up it begins to ring. She answers on the third ring; her soft, sleepy voice saying, "Hello?" *Christ, why the hell did I do this? I have no business dragging her down with me.* "Hello?" There's a short pause, then she whispers, "Liam, is that you?"

Closing my eyes, I grip my hair tightly. "Yeah…I'm sorry I woke you."

"That's okay. Are you all right?" I can't answer her; can't lie to her… can't do anything but sit here and let my uncertainty eat me up. "Liam, please talk to me. Let me help you."

"I don't want to do this."

"Don't want to do what? Don't want to tell me something? Don't want to be with me? Walk away? What?"

"All of the above," I reply.

I can't miss her shaky, inhaled gasp that echoes accusingly through the phone. "Okay. That's a good start. What don't you want to tell me?"

I stare over at Faith's picture. "I don't want to tell you about her."

"Okay. But I think you need to. So when you're ready, you tell me. I'll listen. No judgment, no questions. Just listening."

"Okay."

"So, you don't want to be with me?"

I groan into the receiver. "Of course I want to be with you."

"Well that's good at least." She pauses for minute, then, "So, then you don't want to walk away?"

"God no. That's the last thing I want."

"Then talk to me Liam. Tell me what haunts you." I hear her shaky, inhaled breath. "Tell me about Faith."

I'm not shocked that she knows her name, though knowing Grace I'm sure any information Emma has asked for has been locked down tight. Grace is many things – brash, outspoken, persistent - but she's the most loyal person in the world. She'd never betray me by telling someone about my history with Faith. She'd never betray Faith by talking about her to a stranger either.

"She was the love of your life." Emma says this without asking, like she already knows the truth and just needs my...confirmation.

"Yeah, she was."

"And she died."

Her blunt words hit me right in the gut; right where all the pain is centered. "Yeah, she did."

"And you can't move forward with me because you still love her."

She's shockingly direct and very close to the truth. "I do love her. I always will."

"Okay."

I get to my feet and take the picture off the wall. "I have loved her my entire life, from the first moment I laid eyes on her when I was twelve." I chuckle. "Kinda weird, I know."

She laughs. "No, I think it's sweet."

"Well anyway, so we didn't get together until a few years before.... well...um...before I lost her." Saying the words out loud still kill me; saying the word 'died' is something I'm rarely able to do. "We had plans, lots of plans. We were gonna travel the world, we were gonna get married in some crazy place like the rainforest. And then she got sick." I flop down onto the bed. "She was so young, just twenty-five, so at first the fucking doctors didn't believe her when she said she felt a lump." I gaze into Faith's beautiful, smiling face reflected back at me. "She was so strong, right up until the end."

"Tell me more about her Liam. I want to know her."

I'm shocked at her ability to not lay the pity on thick, like most people do. Sure, it's in our nature to express sympathy, but it's the thing I hate the most; those fucking pitiful looks people give me when they find out she's gone, and the unsettling way they try to express their sorrow....stumbling over stupid words that really make no difference at all. Nothing anyone will ever say to me will change the fact that she was taken too soon.

So I spend a good thirty minutes just talking about her; about her friendship with Grace, her contagious laugh, her easy-going attitude. Emma stays mostly silent; snickering occasionally and making a few comments but generally just letting me talk.

Then I start telling her about how sick Faith was, and how I cared for her daily the last six months of her life. I lived at her parent's house, slept in a sleeping bag next to her bed and never once left her side. I carried her to the bathroom, held the bucket while she puked, and drove her to endless doctor's appointments. I did anything and everything to make her fight bearable; did anything I could to give her strength.

In the end, nothing I did made any difference. Cancer was the boss; it was in charge. And all I could do was sit back and watch as each day she was taken from me a little at a time. "The last thing she ever said to me was I love you." I roll my eyes to the ceiling; ignore the tears that are sliding down my face. "I'm so grateful and thankful for that."

There are long moments of silence between us and the muffled sound of sobbing. What little I've learned about Emma in these past few days, I know that her heart is not only breaking for me, but for the amazing girl she never got to meet. I've never been so grateful for a new friendship since the one I had with Faith.

"Thank you for telling me about her," Emma whispers once we're both able to talk again.

"Thanks for listening."

"I get it now Liam. I understand why sometimes even the idea of us together is just too much for you to handle. And I would completely understand if you feel like you need to walk away before we get any closer. I would never want to hurt you or cause you anymore pain."

"Ah babe, the last thing I want to do is walk away. I've just gotta figure out how to do this, without all the shit from my past getting in the way." I set Faith's picture down on the nightstand. "In the meantime, I'd like us to continue to get to know one another, be friends, if that's okay with you."

She snickers. "Um…yeah, that's more than okay with me."

I chuckle. "Well that's good to know."

"Are you gonna be okay? Do you want me to come over?"

Images flash in my head; pictures I'm sure she has no idea that I think about on a daily basis. Pictures of us together…minimal or no clothing…. doing unspeakable things to one another's bodies. "Uh…yeah, I'd love for you to come over. But I don't think it's a wise idea. Us in a room with a bed….bad, bad idea."

She gasps at my bold words, then starts to laugh. "Yeah, I suppose you're right."

There's a few more minutes of silence, just us sitting there together absorbing what's been said, listening to one another breathing. I finally feel a resemblance of peace and think that maybe, just maybe, I'll be able to sleep tonight. "I'm gonna go Em. I'll see you in the morning."

I feel her smile through the phone. "Um, you mean in a few hours."

I glance at the clock and snicker, "Yeah, in a few hours." I roll to the side, click the light off. "Sweet dreams."

"You too Liam."

CHAPTER 8

I do manage to actually sleep, and would have slept through my alarm if my irritating sister hadn't called. I spend a minute or two berating her for her early morning annoyance, and once she's reassured that I have not completely lost my mind in the past twenty-four hours, she signs off; not, of course, until after she informs me what she plans on doing to Ryan to wake him up.

God I hate her.

I take a quick shower and drag on clean clothes; save the caffeine fix for the good stuff that I'll get at Emma's place. I'm out the door minutes later, and I refuse to admit how anxious I am to see her.

I suppose I should be embarrassed, since I did spew the mother-load out of my trap last night. But for some reason, I'm not. I'm relieved; really, really relieved actually. Letting go of some of the pain and allowing Emma in has given me a weird sense of freedom that I didn't even realize I needed; which is what I concentrate on while I drive.

The scents coming from the inside of the café tell me that she's been here baking for quite a while. The music is up loud, since the café is not yet open, so she doesn't hear me come through the door; which gives me a prime opportunity to linger in the kitchen doorway and just watch her.

As usual, her hair is up; piled high up on her head with a few stray strands escaping to curl down around her face. Her ratty old t-shirt is too tight, hugging her slim frame and full chest like a second skin. The denim shorts are tattered and too short and definitely not what she usually wears to work. She's either trying to drive me crazy or she just rolled out of bed and came on in. Either way, I'm not complaining, but keeping my hands to myself is most certainly going to be a challenge; especially when she starts moving her hips to the beat coming from the speakers.

Good God, this woman is gonna drive me to start drinking…again. Resisting her is not something I'm sure I can do, and since the blood has all raced from my brain and is now centered in my dick, I'm not sure I can even think of a good reason to stay away.

Emma gyrates across the room, sheet pan in hand. Once she shoves it into the oven she turns; her eyes instantly finding mine and all motion coming to a halt. Of course, that's only brief, because she takes off running across the room and launches herself into my arms. She hits my chest with a solid thud; her arms wrapping tightly around my neck.

Laughing I say, "Well, hello to you too." I'm holding her a good foot off the ground, her legs dangling in mid-air.

"I'm so glad you're here," she replies.

Frowning, I ask, "Did you think I wasn't coming in?"

She shrugs. "I wasn't sure. Last night was pretty intense."

I boost her up, lock my hands on her ass and ease her legs around my hips. I'm certain I must be a glutton for punishment. "Yeah, it was." I press my lips to her forehead. "Thank you for that, by the way."

"For what?"

My eyes travel over her face, see the tiredness centered in her eyes. "For listening, for being there." I tug her closer, hope she can't feel the effect she's having on me. "Just for being you."

Her grin lights up her face. "You're welcome." Her eyes search my face, linger on my lips, then she's back looking in my eyes once again. "You look tired."

"So do you," I reply. "Did you sleep at all?"

She shakes her dark head. "Nope. I just decided to come in."

I frown at her. "You've been here all night?"

"Wouldn't be the first time."

"Babe, that's not very safe," I urge.

Her laughter fills the room. "Liam, I've been doing this for over five years. I've pulled a lot of all-nighters." Her flour-covered hands cup my face. "I'm careful, I promise."

I walk us toward the front of the shop and by the time I'm filling my cup and simultaneously hanging onto to her, she's laughing hysterically and tightening her legs around me. "You must really need coffee," she giggles.

My eyes find hers. "I do. And I really don't need to let you go. Not yet."

Her smile fades and once again her eyes center on my lips. "Um…okay."

I prop her ass on top of the back counter, giving my hands freedom to roam. "So, what's with the sexy outfit?"

She shrugs. "Just what I had on around the house. I brought clothes to change into."

I grin at her and grasp her ass in my palms. Just as I thought long ago, it's a perfect fit. "Please don't. You look very….hot."

Her laughter rings out again. "You're crazy. I look like a slob."

"Far from it, I'm sure," I state, offering her my cup and tipping it up just enough for her to sip from. Who would have thought that something as mundane as sharing a cup of coffee could be such a turn on?

Oh fuck, who am I kidding? Emma could stand on her head and scream and I'd find something sexy about it.

"I gotta open soon," she says, her fingers threading through my hair. "You should kiss me now. It's gonna be a long day."

I grin at her. "Oh I should, huh? And you think that's such a good idea?"

She smiles at me. "I most definitely do."

Leaning close, my face an inch away from hers, I whisper, "If I kiss you now, I won't stop. I can't stop."

"Um. Okay. I can be closed today."

Shaking my head, I smirk at her, "Not what I mean Em."

"Oh," she states. "So, you don't want to kiss me?"

I start to laugh. "I want nothing more." I reconsider that thought, then, "Well, actually I want a lot more. But I think we'll settle on this little grab-ass thing we've got going on. It's a good start."

She nods. "Yep. I agree."

I drop a kiss on her forehead, assist her down off the counter and refill my coffee. "So boss, what's on the agenda for today?"

I'm half-listening while she goes through our list of to-dos, following along behind her and sipping at my coffee; my eyes locked firmly on her tight ass and trim legs. A host of brand new X-rated images flash in my head and I'm slowly re-thinking my choice to take things slow. I need to get her naked….now.

"So, you got all that?" she asks, turning to me and picking up the dirty bowls on the counter.

"Uh…what?"

Her eyes find mine, laughter twinkling in the brown depths. "Did you hear anything I said?"

I could lie, which would be easy. Or I could tell the truth, which is difficult….and new….for me. "No. I didn't."

She frowns at me. "Are you okay?"

I grin at her. "I'm fine. I wasn't listening because I was thinking about you. Naked you."

Her face flames and she grins and looks down at her feet. "Oh. Okay."

Stepping toward her, I shove the warning voices aside and reach out to grasp her face in my hands. "I don't want to scare you Emma. But I do want to be honest." Two steps more and we're locked together, her back pressed up against the work bench. "I want you. Probably more than I should. Definitely more than I have the right to."

"I want you too," she whispers.

"But I gotta take this slow. I want this time to be different."

"What do you mean?"

I tear my eyes away from her, unable to look at her while I reveal the sordid side of myself. "Since I lost Faith, I've…." I curse loudly and drop my hands; step away from her and give myself room to breathe. Glancing over, I see that she's patiently waiting for me to finish; her small hands gripping the bowls tightly. "Since then, I've…fuck!" This is so much harder than I thought it would be, stripping myself down in front of her and revealing what kind-of filth I've become.

"It's okay," she urges. "Go on."

"It's not okay!" I snap, dragging my hands through my hair. "After I lost her, I started drinking. A lot, and all the time. And then I started sleeping around…a lot. Too much." I curse again and slump against the wall. "I've had so many one night stands I've lost count. My only goal the past few years has been to get drunk and get laid." I lift my eyes, glance across the room at her, and my stomach shoots up into my throat.

Her face is white, eyes wide with fear and something else undefined; horror or disgust maybe. I watch as she slowly sets the bowls on the work bench, then grips the edge and leans over; head hanging down between her hands. Her voice is so soft, so ragged, and I barely hear when she asks, "Are you still drinking?"

"No. Not like that. I occasionally allow myself one beer, but that's it."

She nods slowly. "And the girls?"

I'm shaking my head and holding back a shudder. "No. Not since October."

Emma turns to face me. "I'm really trying hard to understand this Liam. But you need to understand that I've only ever been intimate with a few people, and I was in a relationship with each of them. This is a lot to take in."

I nod. "I know it is. Sometimes it's pretty hard for me to accept too." I realize then that I'm going to need to give her space; space to absorb what I've told her, space to decide if this is what she wants for herself. "I should probably go."

She shakes her head, but I notice that her eyes are evasive, avoiding me in every way possible. "Please don't. I like having you here."

I'm not altogether certain her choice is a good one…or a wise one… but nonetheless the choice is hers, so I remain silent and turn toward the sink; blast the water on hot and effectively put an end to our suddenly awkward conversation.

Emma is a subdued version of herself for most of the day and remains as detached from me as she used to be; long ago when she used to insult me and get irritated whenever I stepped foot inside her shop. I keep busy with the dishes and the other chores that she leaves for me on a list taped to the wall and for the majority of the day we avoid talking to one another unless it's absolutely necessary. I even leave for a while to get some lunch to avoid her feeling obligated to do it for me like she usually does.

Grace is there when I return and from her curious look I can tell that she's instantly picked up on Emma's dark mood. She gets right to work on her recipes; smartly cuts her usual chatter down to a minimum. The remaining few hours of work is brutal and exhausting and for the first time I'm actually looking forward to closing up shop, heading home and putting some well-deserved distance between me and Emma.

Once the 'closed' sign is up and the door is locked I get right to work on the front. My earphones are plugged in, music blasting in my ears to help drown out the sound of her sad voice that fills my heart with sickness and pain every time I hear it. I am literally counting the minutes until I can leave and yet the thick sense of desolation hangs over me; the feeling that she's gonna let me go before we've even begun is practically a given.

I'm mopping furiously, taking my frustration out on the already clean floor, when I see her move into the room and walk toward me. Her eyes are sad and with each step closer she takes they slowly fill with tears. Knowing instinctively that the end is here, I set the mop aside and pull the earphones out and stash them in my pocket.

"I'll go Em," I reply. "I'm so sorry."

She walks right up to me and loops her arms around my neck, rises up on her toes and whispers, "I don't want you to go."

Pulling her close, I lean down and lock my lips over hers. She sighs and opens her mouth slightly, the only invitation I need. Groaning low in my throat, I deepen the kiss, slide my tongue against hers and feel the kiss center right in my gut. It's a slow, heated meeting of lips and tongues; of hands grasping. Her fingers travel down, grip my shirt tightly as I walk us backward, prop her back against the wall and grip her face in my hands; holding her in place so that I can ravage her mouth properly, the way I've been dying to for months now.

She squirms beneath me, wrapping one leg around mine and tipping her hips up. Reaching down, I palm her ass and pull her in tight; make sure she feels every inch of how much I want her, how much I need her. She moans into my mouth and the kiss gets deeper, harder; tongues pushing and shoving and driving one another to distraction.

"Hey Em, I…."

Grace's voice is like a bucket of ice water being poured over us. Lifting my head, I glare over at my sister and growl, "Go away."

Grace grins. "Oops. Sorry for the interruption. But the timer is going off and we need to get the next batch going." She laughs. "How much time do you need big brother?"

"Go away!"

She chuckles again. "What's the matter? Having a *hard* time getting your work done?" She laughs louder at her over-emphasis on the word as she walks back into the kitchen.

"Go fuck yourself," I call after her, then glance down at Emma. Her lips are red and swollen from our kiss, her dark eyes hazy with need. Leaning down toward her ear, I whisper, "I hate her."

Emma laughs. "No you don't." Her fingers weave in my hair. "We should probably stop anyway."

I nod. "Yeah." It's not what I want, and I'm certain it's not what she wants either. The look in her eyes, the movement of her hips against mine, the way she keeps looking at my lips, all tell me she wants to strip me bare and have her way with me.

Christ. Like I need that image in my head.

She moves again, sliding herself against the rigid evidence of my need for her. I curse under my breath, slam by mouth against hers for a hot, brief minute, then pull away just enough to remark, "You're pushing me woman."

Her soft sigh against my lips is almost as intoxicating as her rubbing against me. "I really want you."

My eyes meet hers and I slide my hand down between our bodies, cupping her warmth through the worn denim and causing her eyes to darken with need. "I want you too. Just not here. Not now. With my goddamn sister in the other room listening to every word."

Emma grins at me and shamelessly moves against my hand. "I can be quiet."

"Fuck," I growl, sliding my mouth to her ear. "I don't want you quiet. I want you screaming."

She moans and her small fingers dig into my arms. "Anything else you want?" I can tell by the way she's moving, holding me, my words are gonna send her over the edge. It's a far cry from where we were a few hours ago when we did everything to avoid one another. Now we're seconds away from me giving her an orgasm and trying to figure out the quickest way to get her alone.

My tongue traces the curve of her ear and my free hand slides up to cup her breast. "I want you wet with need for me, from my hands, my mouth." Another long, low almost silent moan escapes her lips. "Then I want to slide into you, hard and deep, over and over again." My hand moves fast, increasing the pace that I instinctively know she needs. "I want to make you come."

That's all she needs to send her flying; fingers digging painfully into my skin, face shoved into my chest to muffle the noises I know she wants to make. *Quiet, my ass.* This girl is a screamer...probably a biter too.... and most definitely everything I'll ever need to satisfy me, that's for sure.

Faith's face flashes in my head; a long ago first time, her voice calling out, begging me to come with her, to give her all of myself. We were impatient with one another, foregoing the foreplay that we'd actually been doing for years, and going right into the act itself. I remember thinking that I'd never need anything more.

Shoving the painful thoughts aside, I force myself to concentrate on the beautiful girl in my arms as she comes down from her high. Her face is flushed and her breathing is ragged, and when she looks up at me I see a trust there I hadn't seen before. Betrayal slams into me, hot and fierce and proud. Here she is, falling apart in my arms; and still I'm thinking about someone else.

"Thank you," she laughs exhaustedly. "Guess I needed that."

I pull her close into a hug to avoid having to look at her; use the few brief minutes to get my shit back in order. "Yeah, I guess you did."

"Are you done yet?" Grace hollers from the kitchen. "Haven't you two ever heard of a quickie for crying out loud? Let's get moving."

We both start to laugh, and Grace's interruption is just what I needed to get my feet back on the ground and tamper by racing libido. "I'm gonna kill her. You know that, right?"

Emma sets both feet on the floor. "No you won't. You love her. Even if she is a pain in the butt."

"I can hear you!"

We laugh again and I drop a brief kiss on her lips before I take a few steps back and pick-up the mop. "Go on. Let me finish here."

She squeezes my hand once. "Okay."

I watch her walk away and once she's out of sight I slump back against the wall and blow out the breath I didn't realize I'd been holding. How is it possible to be completely undone by one woman and still have thoughts and memories about the other? I mean yeah...I have thought about Faith off and on when I've been with my one-nighters, but it's never in a lovingly reminiscent way; it's more of a 'wow she would hate this part of me' way. I've never compared those women with Faith because, quite frankly, there was no comparison. Faith was extraordinary, and those women were just an outlet, plain and simple.

To say that I'm torn is an understatement. I want Emma; I haven't wanted someone this much since I wanted Faith way back when. I haven't needed someone this much since I needed Faith; in that almost desperate and clingy way that used to drive her wild. But I don't want to compare the two women; that isn't fair to Faith's memory or at all to Emma. They are both amazing in completely different ways.

Faith was amazing, I correct myself.

Maybe slowing things down is a good thing. When I finally do sleep with Emma I don't want anything between us except skin. No past memories, no certain redhead, no what-ifs or what could have beens.

Emma deserves more than that, and really, so do I.

++++++++++++++++++++

73

The four of us have dinner together later than night and amazingly I actually manage to make it through the entire evening without another freak-out. Grace is on fire....teasing Emma and I about our 'ass-grabbing', as she refers to it. Emma is red-faced, I'm pissed and Ryan just sits back and laughs. I have no idea what all Grace heard, but I can only hope that if she did hear everything, for Emma's sake, she keeps it to herself.

After dinner they invite us back to their apartment to watch a movie, but Emma begs off, saying she's tired and I'm anxious to get home and get some breathing room from all that happened today. Sadly, I admit to myself that I also need some time away from being with Emma, tempting though she is. It all is so new and different from anything I've experienced in the past few sleazy years, and it's all just a little too much to wrap my brain around.

We head out to our cars together and after Grace and Ryan take off I walk Emma to her compact. Our hands are looped together, as they have been for most of the night; the feeling oddly natural and very comfortable. Too comfortable, I think as my stomach rolls nervously. "I need to do some laundry and stuff tomorrow. But I'll be in around lunch to get caught up on the dishes and help with closing." I hope she doesn't see through my excuse; that I really need some distance now, even though I can't fully explain it...even to myself.

Her eyes find mine and a soft smile lights her face. "Take tomorrow off. Grace is coming in and we can handle it. Besides, you have work on Monday. You need to rest up."

She's giving me the out I need, and although I know she doesn't see the truth in it, maybe she needs a break from me too. "You sure?"

She nods. "I'm sure."

I pull her close, hug her tightly to my chest. "Get some rest. I'll call you tomorrow."

"I'd like that."

Taking a step back, I set her aside; force myself not to kiss her goodbye. I want to kiss her, more than she probably knows, but what I need more than that kiss are a few minutes to just.....breathe. "Drive safe."

"You too."

Once I'm in my truck I sigh with relief; which immediately is followed by a wave of guilt. I don't want to be relieved to be apart from Emma, but everything about her, whether she realizes it or not, pushes me to go to a place I'm not yet capable of being. It's not anything she says or does;

in fact it's probably more in my head than anything. But being with her challenges me; it forces me to admit my downfalls, admit my mistakes, and admit what I want....which, for the past few years now I've managed to avoid completely. Drunkenness and anonymous pussy will do that for you.

The blinders are off now. And what I want is a question I'm asking myself daily; a question Emma will soon be asking as well. For now, she seems content to just roll along with things....taking things slow, and when they heat up allowing me to back off once again. But at what point will that not be enough for her? At what point will she demand more, because she can or because she should? At what point will she require more from me that I'll ever be able to give?

I guess I need to figure out how to accept what we have together and just take each day as it comes. The challenges, when they happen, I'll have to deal with. For now, I know I need to work on not letting Faith pop up every time something with Emma reminds me of the past. Emma deserves better; so does Faith.

CHAPTER 9

Now that I'm back at work life feels more normal. As usual, my hours are excruciating, which leaves me no time to see Emma and minimal time to dwell on her or anything else that clogs up my head unnecessarily. I do try to call her almost every night, but sometimes she's busy at the café or with her family or I'm just too tired to do anything more than say a few words.

Saturday morning I stop by early on my way to work, eat two of her amazing cannoli then pull her into the kitchen and kiss her senseless before I leave. Like the week before, we meet up with Grace and Ryan for dinner later that night, and this time Moose and his on-again girlfriend Autumn join us.

I attempt to spend the following day at home, forcing myself not to go to the café; forcing myself to give the two of us the space that we need to build this relationship slowly. I putter around, clean up the apartment, do some laundry and give my dad a call.

By noon I'm going nuts. I want to see her. I want to hang out in the cafe with her, doing dishes and just talking about nothing. I want to be with her, even if I know that I may end up feeling anxious and needing a break later on.

So I shower and change and head out; force myself not to speed to get to my destination. By the time I pull into the parking lot, shut the truck off and speed walk to the café, I can't help but laugh at myself. I feel like a freakin' teenager with a full-on crush.

The café is packed at this hour; late risers and church goers coming in for their caffeine and sugar fix. Emma is behind the counter, chatting away with an elderly couple as she pulls items from the pastry case. Her eyes meet mine and I have no idea what she sees; but her smile widens and she gives me a wink.

Yep…it centers right in my jeans.

I head into the kitchen, find my sister elbow deep in flour, and growl, "Can you cover the front for a minute. I need to talk to Emma."

She glances up at me and a knowing smirk lights her face. "You don't need to talk to her Liam. You just want to fuck her."

I shove the images in my head aside and stomp toward her. "Grace, if you ever loved me at all, you'll do this for me."

She laughs and starts to slap the flour off her hands. "I got you covered big brother."

It feels like hours from the time she scrubs herself clean to when she heads out front to get Emma. Then there's a few long painful minutes where I wait; I wait and listen and watch the clock and silently beg for her to hurry up and get her ass back here.

When Emma finally walks into the room, I take her hand and pull her toward the back door, where we'll be semi-hidden by the large proofing racks. Her eyes are wide, curious and filled with need as I shove her against the supply closet door and wrap her in my arms.

"I really need to kiss you," I growl. I don't give her time to answer or protest, just slam my mouth down on hers and go in search of her tongue. Her soft moan greets me and she slides her small hands down my back, cupping my ass tightly. Her need is palatable and if we were alone I wouldn't hesitate to yank our jeans down and slide into her again and again.

But the voices from just outside the kitchen doorway remind me that we are most definitely not alone and this is not the time and place for what I want to accomplish. It sure as hell does not allow me the amount of time I require to satisfy the need I have for her.

I lift my mouth, nibble softly on her bottom lip. "I really needed that."

"Me too," she whispers, one hand sliding under my t-shirt and scorching a path up my back.

Leaning my forehead against hers, I force my breathing to slow and slide my hands up and down her curves. "I'm here to work."

She chuckles. "Is that so?"

I shrug. "Well, I might sneak in some…other stuff….too."

A wide grin lights her face. "I hope so." Her lips press against mine once….twice…and on the third pass her tongue strokes a path over my lips.

I growl under my breath. "Christ woman, do you know what you do to me?"

One small hand slides down between our bodies and she gives me a squeeze. "Absolutely."

I grasp her hand in mine, blow out a shaky breath and stare up at the ceiling; count the tiles slowly one by one to take my mind off of all the things I want to do to her.

"Sorry guys, but it's getting kinda crazy out here. And the case needs to be filled," Grace calls from the doorway.

I take a step back, still staring at the ceiling and now tearing at my hair. Emma pats me on the chest, presses her lips against my neck and scoots out from our hidden spot. When she's gone, I blow out another breath and slump back against the door.

It takes some more deep breathing, some mumbling to myself and a complete inventory of the items I see around the kitchen to tamper down my need and get my body moving. I dive into the massive pile of dishes; grateful for the distraction, although at this point even sudsy dish water emits some type of sexual image in my head.

Music is blasting in my ears, a good diversion from the crazy thoughts racing forward. I need to get my shit together, otherwise I'm gonna scare the poor girl to death. It's bad enough that I came in here earlier like a crazy man; hell bent on getting what I want and refusing to take no for answer.

By the time we close for the afternoon I'm relatively back on earth where I should be. Grace keeps snickering whenever she looks at me and Emma just moves around like she usually does; doing three things at once and making it all look so easy.

I leave the girls to finish baking while I clean the front; dawdle as long as I can to avoid having to tell her goodbye. When I eventually return to the kitchen, Grace is heading out and Emma is pulling off her apron and gripping it between her fingers.

"See you guys," Grace calls with a wave over her shoulder. Emma and I murmur something to her, but we continue to stare at one another from across the work bench.

Emma's dark eyes are locked on mine as she stashes the apron with all the other dirty laundry, then slowly walks around the bench until she's standing directly in front of me. "I need you Liam."

I had myself prepared for a lot of things, but I never thought she'd come right out and say the words that have been on the tip of my tongue for weeks now. "You sure about that Em?"

She nods. "Absolutely." I watch as she kicks off her sneakers, then reaches down, unzips her jeans and slides them to the floor.

Frowning, shaken and caught completely off-guard, I grumble, "What? Here?"

She nods. "Yep. Here. Now. Anywhere." Her t-shirt soon follows and before I can blink she's standing in front of me in a barely there thong and lacy bra.

"Holy fuck Em." That tiny little body of hers is curvy in all the right places; tan, flat stomach….round hips…..and rosy nipples that peek through the lace and are begging for my attention.

With one quick yank my shirt joins the ever-growing pile of clothes and I can't help but smile when I see the grin light her face; apparently she appreciates all the manual labor I do each day. I make quick work of my shoes, socks and jeans and when I'm standing next to her in just boxer briefs we both start to laugh at the absurdity of the situation.

"Sure you don't want to take this somewhere that has a bed?" I ask, pulling her close and wrapping my arms around her.

"Maybe later." Her eyes lock onto mine. "Right now I just need you in me."

I'm slightly shocked at this forwardness from her; shocked….and completely turned on. I reach for the snap on her bra, undo it and slide the straps down her arms. She's gorgeous, perfect in every way and my mouth is watering as I bend down and draw one tight, rosy nipple in between my lips. She moans loudly, all the affirmation I need to slide her thong down her legs and stroke my fingers between them.

She's wet with need for me already and I can feel my patience taking a back seat to my urgent strive to bury myself in her. I stroke her a few times, then slide a finger deep…oh so easily. She moans again, whispers something into my hair and reaches to pull down my briefs. Torn between wanting to be bare and wanting to keep my hand in her, we work together to pull them down and once I kick the shorts aside I'm back with her completely.

My teeth tug and pull at her nipples and she writhes against me, calling out my name and muttering incoherent words. Her hands reach out, stroke me firmly until I finally have to take her wrists and stop her, panting, "We gotta slow down. I wanna be in you when I come."

Her dark, needy eyes flash to mine. "Then hurry up already."

I chuckle, disengage my body from hers and retrieve a condom from my wallet. She watches me closely as I tear open the wrapper and roll it on; her dark gaze and firm pink nipples a huge turn on. Once I'm set, I lift her up and with her legs wound around my hips walk us toward the wall; not the perfect spot for this, but I can't imagine dirtying up her work bench with....everything.

My eyes are locked on hers as I hold her thighs tight and tip my hips up; sliding slowly into her body. She's scorching hot, tight as a vice and slick with need and I can't help but groan at how exquisite she feels.

"Ah...Christ Em....that's good."

Once I'm buried as deep as possible, I just stay there; letting her get used to the feel of me, the feel of us together. When she whimpers I take that as my cue to move; pull almost all the way out and slide back in. I go slowly at first, enjoying the amazing sensations of her body, the panting breath against face, the nails digging into my shoulders.

"Liam?" she whispers.

I surge harder, deeper....setting the perfect pace for her and for me. Pulling back slightly, I gaze down at her; eyes now closed, her face a mixture of pleasure and agony, those perfect upturned breasts bouncing with each thrust. Then I look further, to where are bodies are joined; watch as I slide so effortlessly into her again and again. The sight is erotic and almost my undoing and without another thought I'm thrusting harder, faster and pushing us both toward the top.

When I manage to look up she's staring at me, her teeth locked on her lower lip as she groans, "Please...."

"Please what babe? Tell me what you need."

"I need to come," she whimpers.

Leaning forward, I take her mouth in mine, kiss her senseless for a moment and gently slow the pace. Then I pull my mouth away, just enough so that we're close but not touching. "Look down. Watch me make you come." I pick up the pace once more, pull back just enough so that she can do as I requested. I keep my hands locked on her hips as I thrust hard and hear her start to moan. "That's it baby." She's digging her nails into my arms, tightening her legs around my hips, when I feel her body begin to shake; her tight sheath grips me hard as the orgasm hits. Like I predicted, she screams out her release; arching her back and begging for me to join her.

I'm completely done. With two more deep thrusts I'm coming hard, growling out her name into her hair and gripping her hips tight with my fingers. We're panting and sweating and moaning and I can barely remain upright I'm so torched by my orgasm. She's still shaking in my arms, the after-effects still rocketing through her body, soft moans echoing from her mouth in between kisses she trails down my neck.

When I can eventually think coherently, I lift my head and look at her and we both start to laugh uncontrollably. Here we are, in the middle of what's supposed to be a sanitary space; clothes strewn all over, our sweaty bodies propped up against a wall between the makeshift desk and dishwasher. It's certainly not romantic, but it's definitely one of the best things I've ever experienced.

A memory flashes through my head; Faith and I in her parent's garage, pants down around our ankles as we fuck against her dad's old Buick. She'd been between treatments….feeling good that day…and needing me. But her overprotective parents wouldn't let her leave the house, so that was our solution….find some place semi-private and go for it.

That was the last time we were ever together physically, before she was taken from me forever.

"Liam? You okay?"

Emma's soft voice breaks through my daydreaming and as shaken as I am by the old memory, I force a neutral expression. "Uh…yeah…I'm good."

She frowns. "You sure? Cuz you just stopped laughing and stared off into space."

I nod. "Yep. I'm good." The lie hovers in the air around us and I'm certain she can see the truth, although she seems to take it in stride as I disengage our bodies and turn to dispose of the condom.

We dress in silence and then she turns to me with a wide smile and weaves her arms around my waist. "So, feel like going out for dinner?"

What I really want to is to hightail it out of here, give the two of us some space and give myself a minute to breathe. The urge to flee, to hide, is eating at me and as the minutes go by I'm having a difficult time shoving those needs aside and doing what's right for Emma.

Small hands cup my face and gently pull me down. She brushes her lips against mine once, then pulls back enough to whisper, "It's okay Liam. You can talk to me about whatever is going on inside your head."

She has this eerie knowledge of how I work and I have no idea how she's managed to figure me out; but she has. Looking down at her, I don't see the anger that I expect or even the jealousy that she's entitled. I see only the concern from a person who cares about me.

"There are just times….when you and I are together….that remind me of when…of when…."

"We remind you of you and Faith. Is that what you're saying?"

I shrug. "Yeah. Sometimes we do. And other times, not at all. You and she are different, but…it's just that….fuck." I'm frustrated because the words I want to say will hurt her. And I want to avoid that more than anything. She deserves so much better than all this; so much more than me, that's for sure.

Her hands thread through my hair. "Go ahead. Tell me."

I gaze over the top of her head, at the oven on the back wall. "The similarities that are there are not so much about you two girls, but about the relationship. A lot of what I'm feeling now, I felt then, when Faith and I first got together. And it scares the hell out of me."

"Scares you because you're afraid of feeling it again or because your first instinct is to run from it?"

I lock my eyes on hers. "Because my first instinct is to run. To get as far away from you and all this as possible." I pull out of her arms and move across the room, shove my hands into my pockets. "I don't know if I can do this. I sure as hell can't go through another loss again. I can't do it Em. I just can't. I haven't really even survived her yet."

She nods and blinks furiously to avoid tears. "So, are you saying that as much as you want this…us…it can't happen?"

"I wish I could say that. It would be easier." I take a step toward her. "Sticking it out, hanging in there and fighting for us is gonna be hard. Hell, it's gonna be more than that. It's gonna be brutal….for both of us." Reaching out, I grasp her fingers in mine. "I can't make you any promises, not now at least. And if that's not enough for you, I will completely understand."

Emma nods. "Can we just give it a try? See how things go?"

It's what I want, what I feel like I can handle, but I immediately see how she's getting the raw end of the deal. "Only if you think it will be enough for you."

"Are you going to see other people?"

I wrinkle my face. "God no. That's not what this is about."

She forces a smile. "Oh. Well, okay."

Pulling her into my arms, I blow out a sigh of relief; although I'm not certain relief is what I should be feeling. I have a hunch we are going to continue to have these types of conversations and I just wonder when she's finally going to have had enough of playing second fiddle to a ghost.

++++++++++++++++++++

We end up back at her place, an upscale condominium that makes my trashy apartment look like I live in the slums. She's silent as she pulls me up the stairs and into her large master bedroom; still silent as she strips the clothes from my body, then does the same with hers.

She's not silent when I put my mouth on her skin or tease my way between her legs with my tongue. She's a hotbed of need; tearing at my hair with her fingers when I thrust my tongue in deep and calling out my name when she comes. She's still shaking when she rolls me over and grinds down on my cock; that beautiful body of hers using mine to her every advantage. We come together, just as we did earlier in the evening; surging into one another and moaning loudly.

When she eventually rolls off me and flops onto her side of the bed, I can instantly feel the ice centering between us. I can only chalk it up to the lingering after-effects of the intense conversation we had back at the café.

"Do you want me to stay?" I ask softly. I'm pretty positive everything at this point will require my permission; it's just that tentative and unsure between us now.

"I do." She blows out a breath. "But you should go."

This time I'm the silent one. I sit upright and don't dare look at her as I tug on my clothes. Once my shoes are on, keys are in hand and I'm at the bedroom door, I glance over my shoulder. She hasn't moved an inch and is just lying there with her arms spread wide staring at the ceiling. She looks small and lost in that big bed; not at all like the vivacious woman I've grown to know and care about over the past few months.

I've done this to her, I admit to myself as my stomach rolls nervously. With my barrage of memories and my boat load of shit, I've dumped my crap right on her, right on her shoulders so she can carry the weight of it all. Now she's left with the burden; the burden of choice, the burden to send me packing, the burden that she may be the one to finally break me for good this time. I've sure as hell done a fine job of trying to break her.

In three long strides I'm back on the bed, lying directly on top of her body and staring her directly in the eye. "Talk to me Em. Tell me what you're thinking."

When her eyes meet mine I'm shocked at the emptiness I see there; the emptiness I put there. "I'm thinking that I wish I'd never met you."

Can't say I blame her. There are days I feel exactly the same. "What else?"

Tears fill her eyes. "I'm thinking that I know you're gonna break my heart. You sorta already have."

Leaning down, I kiss away the tears that begin to stream down her face. "I don't want to hurt you. And I meant what I said earlier, I will understand if this is not enough for you."

"I need some time," she whispers shakily.

I nod. "Okay. Take as long as you need. You know where to find me." My lips brush against hers briefly, and then I pull away and get to my feet; pull the covers over her delectable body and turn the bedside light off. I'm barely out of the room before I hear the sobbing begin. The sound echoes in my head long after I've let myself out the front door and am sitting behind the wheel.

I'm at Grace's apartment before I even realize where I'm going. I pound on her door a few times, and when she opens it instead of Ryan I realize that she's probably been expecting me all along.

Her blue eyes skirt up and down my rumple frame. "Sit down. You look awful."

"Thanks," I reply, taking a spot on the couch.

She hands me a beer…gives me her token stink-eye…. then curls up in the Lazy-Boy and says, "Okay. What's going on with you and Em?"

My fingers tear through my hair. "Christ, I've fucked it up. Of course."

She frowns. "How did you fuck it up?" She sips at her beer and waits patiently while I dig around in my head for the right words to say.

"Well…we…um…" I swear loudly and chug half the beer.

Grace blows out a heavy, annoyed breath and grumbles, "You fucked her."

"Jesus Grace," I growl.

She shrugs. "Well, you did, didn't you?"

I nod. "Yeah. I did." I blow out a breath and lean my head back against the couch. "I keep having flash backs…memories…whatever….of times I was with Faith. But now I have them when I'm with Em."

"Ah shit…you didn't…." she snaps.

"I did." I roll the bottle between my hands. "It was after, but still….I froze up like I did that night at dinner. She knew something was wrong and we talked. Now it's all out there and I think I've lost her."

"You're rambling Liam."

"Fuck! I know that!" I get to my feet and pace the small distance from the living room to the kitchen and back. "I was honest with her Grace, about it all. How being with her reminds me of when I was first with Faith. How some of the stuff is similar. And I even told her that she scares me… that us together…scares me. I told her that if she needs more or if this is too much for her, I'd understand if she wants to walk away."

"So, what did she say?"

"That's just it; she didn't say a whole lot. It's like she disappeared. She got all quiet and we went to her place and…." I swear under my breath and tear my fingers through my hair.

"Fucked."

I roll my eyes at my sister. "Christ…really?"

Grace laughs. "It's Ryan's fault." Then she waves her hand at me, motioning for me to continue.

"Yes, we went back to her place and had sex. And she was just…going through the motions. She was just….so…lost."

"Ah Liam, I'm so sorry."

I look at my sister; into the same blue eyes I see in the mirror each day. "How do I fix this Gracie? How do I build something with her and deal with the shit from Faith, and still not lose my mind?"

Grace shrugs. "I have no idea. By talking to her about what's going on inside your head, I guess. By telling her how you feel about her." She frowns. "How do you feel about her?"

"I have no clue." I resume my seat on the couch. "Obviously, I'm attracted to her."

"Yes, by all the fucking, we've established that," Grace smirks.

I throw her a scowl. "And I really like just being around her. Hanging out at the café or going to dinner with you guys. She's cool and we have fun together."

Grace cocks her head and gives me a pointed look. "So, let me get this straight. You have fun with her, you can talk to her and you like to fuck her, but you have no idea how you feel. Is that about right?"

It all sounds ridiculous when she puts it out there like that. "Yeah, that's right."

She starts to laugh. "Jesus Liam, you care about the girl. And what's not to like? She's beautiful, she's smart, she's a got a hot body, and her own business." Grace grins and raises one eyebrow. "If I wasn't taken I'd fuck her."

"I heard that!" Ryan's voice bellows from the bedroom.

She leans over and whispers loudly. "He likes to fantasize about me with other women."

I start to laugh. "You are crazy little sister, you know that?"

She wiggles her eyebrows up and down. "I may be, but I have a rockin sex life."

Rolling my eyes, I get to my feet and set the beer on the coffee table. "I'm gonna take off. Let you get back to whatever it was you were doing."

Her grin tells me I don't want to know, but she blurts out, "Oh, I was just sucking…"

"Stop! Don't tell me!" I hug her briefly. "You are such a little tramp."

"I know. Ryan loves me that way."

"See ya man," I yell down the hall. "Sorry for the interruption."

"It's all good. Take it easy."

Grace walks me to the door. "Liam, give yourself a little latitude about all this. You can't expect to have no memories of Faith. And of course, the first real relationship you have is gonna drag all that stuff up. That's a good thing. You and Faith were in love and you had a beautiful relationship and a great, long friendship. It's unrealistic to assume you won't think about her again just because she's gone. If that's what Emma expects, she may not be the one for you."

I nod. "Yeah, you're right. You're always right. Dammit."

The shit-eating grin is back. "I'm also very horny. So get the hell out of here so I can go fuck Ryan."

"Christ Grace! Is it really necessary to tell me that?"

She shrugs. "No. I just like messing with you."

I drop a kiss on her forehead. "I love you."

"Love you too Liam."

Now that I'm calmed down and have talked this out with Grace, I want nothing more than to go to Emma, pull her into my arms and just hold her. I'm sure that's the last thing she wants now, but I need her to know that I'm thinking about her. So before I can give it any further thought, I fire off a text, then put my truck in gear and head for home. I doubt I'll hear from her; tonight or any time soon. I know she needs time to figure out where I stand in her life; time to figure out if she needs to let me go for good. The thought of never seeing her again scares me; in ways I never thought possible.

Just as I'm going through the front door my phone buzzes, alerting me to an incoming message. I wait to read it until I'm in bed; swipe my finger across the screen. It says simply, "I miss you too."

CHAPTER 10

I don't hear from Emma for two long weeks. And during that time while I'm waiting….watching my phone….and hoping she'll call, I'm beating myself up for all my shitty choices and for how I've treated her. Thankfully, work keeps me busy; a streak of warm weather dries things up and we're back at it full steam ahead. I'm so busy during the day, with the piles of crap I have to get done in the office, and the little shit I keep getting pulled in to do….help frame this wall….finish the drywall on that one….that I fall into bed each night completely exhausted and unable to give Emma the worry she's due.

Because of that, her face comes to me in dreams; the beautiful eyes filled with light and laughter, then immediately sad and teary, just as they were the night I walked out of her condo. I wake to her voice calling out to me, then realize it's Faith's voice I'm hearing in my head and not Emma's. Time and time again I dream about her lying in the middle of that big bed, arms spread wide in invitation; eyes filled with hate. Everything I dream is a conflict, a barrage of different memories, different faces, all meshed together and overlapping.

I cope with the torrent of dreams and memories like I've coped with most everything the past few years….by drowning my sorrows in alcohol. I hate myself for going there….where I promised myself I wouldn't ever go again. But the demons in my head are not easily silenced, and admittedly drinking is an easy out.

I'm pretty pissed at myself…about most everything. I'm pissed that I've given into my craving; let it be the bandage once again for things I refuse to deal with. I'm pissed that I have let my past influence my future. The one thing I didn't want to do was hurt Emma; I sure as hell have hurt enough people in the past four years and I don't need to add her to the list. But I have hurt her, to what extent I may never know. I hope I get the chance to ask her; hope we can eventually talk some of this shit out and give us a try.

When my phone peels late Saturday night, two excruciating weeks from the last time we spoke, I instantly pick it up and read the text from her. It says only, "I need to talk to you. Please call me."

Now what the fuck am I supposed to do? Calling her sounds ominous to me; like she doesn't want to see me in person to tell me to take a hike. Calling her sounds like an easy way out; she can always hang up on me and not being face to face it will be easy to hide the truth. I know I need to see her, if for nothing else than I need to hear the words right from her mouth; see her intention directly from her eyes.

Grateful that I'm at least sober tonight, I grab up my keys, head to the truck and gun the engine. The drive to her condo takes about ten minutes, and as I pull up in front I'm certain she's not home. Only the porch light is on; all the windows inside are dark, and her car isn't parked in the driveway. I have no doubt about where she is, and to say I'm pissed at her being in her shop this late at night is an understatement.

I curse loudly a few dozen times, then put the truck into gear and drive the five miles to the her café. My stomach tightens with anticipation when I see her car parked outside and all the lights on inside, and when I reach for the front door and find it open that feeling slides away and is replaced once again by a dark surge of anger. It's almost midnight and this is not the best part of town, and yet she's all alone inside with the door unlocked in invitation; just ripe for someone to hurt her.

Locking the door behind me I head to the kitchen, where I hear loud music blaring. Rounding the corner, I see her standing with her back to me at the work bench, shaking her hips and singing loudly to Maroon 5. She's wearing a short dress; those toned, legs of hers doing crazy things to my imagination. As usual, there's flour everywhere; all over the table, her arms and on her neck, where tendrils of her hair are dusted with it too. She's so intoxicating, so incredibly beautiful, I'm almost speechless.

The song ends and immediately starts up again as she crosses the room to retrieve a clean sheet pan. On her return, she startles; sees me standing in the doorway, and I notice that the momentary look of elation is quickly masked with annoyance. Reminds me a lot of how she once used to look at me; back when I irritated the crap out of her and did everything I could to piss her off, just to get a rise out of her.

"What are you doing here?" she asks, avoiding my eyes and resuming her task. "I asked you to call me."

"I know you did," I reply, coming around the bench so that I'm standing directly across from her. "I want you to say whatever you need say directly to my face." She glances up at me, and once again I see her expression change briefly before she hides behind indifference. "If you're gonna tell me to take a hike, I want to hear it in person Em, not on the damn phone."

Her hands still on the dough and she finally raises her eyes to mine. "Is that what you think? That I'm gonna let you go?"

I shrug. "I don't know what to think. But after two weeks of silence I've got a pretty good idea."

"I told you I needed time."

Nodding, I state, "I know you did. And I gave that to you. I'll give you longer if you need it." I hate the idea of that, but at this point I'll do just about anything to have her back in my life.

Icy fear threads through my body at the thought and I force myself to bite it back; hide it however I can. The reality that I am just that desperate to be with her—to be around her on a daily basis—doesn't escape my muddied brain. I haven't felt this type of deep, nagging need for years. Not since I used to run around with Faith, just hoping she'd see me as something more than her friend. I remember the mood swings; elation like no other when she'd graze her hand with mine....to only be followed by perilous doubt and sadness when she informed me she had a new boyfriend.

I really believed when I lost her, I'd never have to feel that way again. And yet, here I stand, basically handing myself over to Emma; leaving the ball entirely in her court and letting her be the deciding factor in my future. As the fear recedes, the anger starts to bubble up once again. Anger at myself, for sounding and acting like a desperate fool. Anger at her, for making me feel like this again. Anger at both of us for thinking we could be anything more than the occasional hot roll in the sack.

She puts the last of the pastries on the sheet pan; wipes her hands and unties the apron. Then she comes around to my side of the table and rests her hands on my chest. "I want to give us a try Liam. I'm scared of it, and of you, but I can't imagine you not being in my life."

I have imagined many words exiting her mouth; leave me alone, I don't want to see you again, stay far away from me....but I never once thought it would be this easy; that I'd just walk in here one day and she'd welcome me with open arms. Especially since the expression on her face is in complete contradiction with her words.

"You sure about that Em, because I'm not convinced." My words are harsh, and yeah...I should tread lightly where she's concerned. But I want her going into this with a clear heart, and open mind; no second thoughts that she might not be making the right choice.

My own second thoughts are more than enough for one relationship.

She nods and takes a step back, her hands falling at her sides. "I do want to try. I know it will be difficult, but I think we're good together."

Shoving my hands in my pockets, I steal myself and ask, "What about...you know....the shit I'm still dealing with?"

She shrugs with forced nonchalance, but I can see the hurt cross her face; the pain that another woman is taking up my headspace. "I guess I'll have to learn to deal with it. I can't expect you not to think about her. She was a part of your life for a very long time."

I nod. "Yeah, that's true."

Emma steps closer, weaves her arms around my neck. "I've missed you Liam. These two weeks have been so difficult. And not one day has gone by when I haven't had to force myself not to call you."

I loop my hands around her waist. "Longest two weeks of my life too Em."

Her fingers thread through my hair, trail down the scruff on my face. "We can do this, can't we?"

"Yeah babe, we can." I wish I felt as self-assured as my words seem to be. The doubts seem to be right there at the surface though, reminding me that this is foreign territory and is going to require me being able to hand myself over to her; body and soul. I wish I could say that I was strong enough to do this without ever looking back; get into this with her without any hesitation. But the lingering doubts...fear....trepidation....all remind me that I'm nowhere near being healed, or free from the memories that haunt me daily.

I am, however, gonna give it a good solid try. She deserves that; deserves more actually. Giving this...us...a chance will be hard; as difficult as some of the shit I've had to deal with the past four years. But I'd have more regrets if I didn't at least give it my best shot and at least try to make her mine; try to make her as happy as she deserves to be.

She rises up on her tiptoes, presses soft, wet kisses on my neck, then up my jaw until our mouths meet. She's hungry for me, immediately deepening the kiss and uttering a soft sigh as she presses her body against mine. Our tongues meet, a heated dual that ignites the fire that's been simmering since we last saw one another. Her hands grip my shirt, slide down and cup my ass before she goes to work on my belt. As she works the button and zipper, her tongue is moving furiously with mine; her teeth nibbling at my lips. She pauses only long enough to reach under her dress and slide her panties down and off, then she's back on me; yanking my jeans and briefs out of the way just enough so that her greedy hands can grasp me firmly.

While she works me up, I somehow manage to extract my wallet and pull out a few condoms from inside. She barely notices; so intent on dragging her tongue down my neck and stroking my rigid flesh that it's almost like she doesn't need me; just the parts of me that will bring her satisfaction....exactly like the last time we were together at her condo.

The lingering anger from earlier surges forward once again and I reach for her hands and lift my head away from hers. Her eyes are wild, hot with need but void of any other emotion; sure as hell not the warm, brown eyes that silently spoke to me the first time we had sex. Her face is flushed, breathing labored, all indications that she's more than ready to set this in motion.

"Why are you stopping?" she asks, though the words come out sounding like a whine.

"Are you sure this is what you want?" Inwardly I'm slapping myself in the head for my ability to think instead of feel. What kind of idiot would put an end to this?

She grins, reaches for my hand and shoves it under her dress. Her skin is damp, heated and more than ready for me. "What do you think?"

"I...I think...." I'm speechless. She has effectively torn me up, with her heated kisses and drenched cleft. Whatever I was going to say can wait.

Up on her toes again, she leans toward my ear and whispers, "I need you Liam."

My mouth slams down on hers again; this time it's me who is hungry, me who is in control. She writhes against my hand, moaning deep within her throat when I begin to rub her swollen clit. Her hands find my cock again, and she grasps tightly and slowly strokes her palm back and forth. Groaning, I tug her hands away and move back just enough to roll the condom into place. Her dark eyes watch me intently; her fingers reaching for the hem of her dress to pull it up and out of the way.

Grasping her none to gently, I turn her to face the work bench and gently push her down, so that she's leaning over slightly and gripping the edges with her fingers. Dragging the dress up until its high on her waist, I slowly trail my palms over her beautiful bare ass, then slide a finger into her sleek warmth.

"Oh….Liam….please….."

I stroke my finger in and out slowly, drawing out the pleasure and heating her up a little each time. Her legs widen, giving me ample room to explore and bring her pleasure. My other hand wraps around in front, working her tight bud with slow circles; bringing her right to the precipice before I stop completely and pull my hands away.

Her head whips around in my direction; eyes wild and angry and needy. "What are you doing? Don't stop."

With my eyes on hers I slide two fingers in, lean over until my cock is pressing hard against her ass. A small smile lifts the corners of her mouth and she sighs with pleasure, moving her hips against me. I'm barely holding on; the need to fuck her, fuck her hard and fast, nagging at my head, my body. I'm almost afraid to be in her now; I'm just that pissed, just that driven to seek my own fulfillment, that I'm worried I'll hurt her.

"Liam…please…now…do it now. God I need you in me," she urges.

Her words are enough to send me over, into that space where I'm only half-existing on the earth; half –existing in my own head. Gripping her hips, I slam in hard; so hard that her entire body jolts and she squeals out her surprise. So hard…that I truly feel like I should apologize for my animal-like behavior. Then she starts to moan…beg for more….over and over again, and any thoughts I might have had about apologizing disappear. I want one thing and one thing only; to fuck her so hard that she'll feel the after effects of me every time she moves.

My pace is relentless and shockingly she keeps right up with me; tipping her hips back to welcome each hard, pounding thrust; urging me on with heated words about what I do to her. It's a short lived union; a few more deep surges in and she's screaming and throwing her head back. I join her almost immediately, with one last brutal jab; emptying myself into the warm, tight glove of her body and growling out my release.

Emma slumps down over the table exhaustedly, panting tiredly while she attempts to regain her composure. Even after all that, I'm still semi-hard; ready for round two and not nearly satisfied enough. Sliding out, I quickly dispose of the condom, then turn her limp body around to face me. Kneeling down, I caress her thighs briefly, then loop one over my shoulder and slowly stroke my tongue gently over her sensitive skin.

"Oh God...Liam...I can't. Not yet."

Ignoring her pleas, I'm hell-bent on my task; dragging my tongue over her swollen flesh, then sliding it deep inside, while my fingers trail up and down her legs. In no time, the tension is leaving her body and she willingly leans down and grips my head; urging me on with her soft moans and rotating her hips against my mouth. It's all the encouragement I need, so I dive right in with a vengeance; sliding my fingers inside and sucking hard on her clit. She's a writhing, squealing ball of need, just as before; and just as before it takes her no time to reach her peak. She lets out a loud moan, a few choice curse words, and tears at my hair as she shakes through her release.

I'm on my feet, condom in place and slamming into her once again before she's even all the way back down. Lifting her up, I set her legs around my waist and prop her against the work bench. Then I'm moving; a man on a mission just as before, gripping her flesh and driving us both toward another mind-blowing orgasm.

When I finally lift my head and look at her, I guiltily realize how I never once considered her comfort. The mad man that I am, I used her body for my own pleasure; regardless of the fact that she's probably now sporting bruises. Our eyes meet, and even though I fully expect to see anger and resentment, all I see is the warmth that was missing when I first walked into the room.

Guilt slams into me head first. "Christ, I'm sorry Em. I have no idea what just happened." My words sound lame and I seriously wish I could call them back and settle for full-on groveling.

Her smile is soft, lazy; a testament to how hard I worked her over. But her hands are gentle as they cup my face and she pulls me down for a kiss. Gone is the anger and hurt from the past few weeks. Gone is the doubt that hovered over me like a cloak. This sweet, soft kiss is an apology....a second chance....maybe even a glimmer of hope that we can make a future together.

When our lips part, we slowly unwind from one another and I set her down on shaky legs. I watch her as I dress; searching the floor for her panties, sliding them back on, which is seriously just as hot as when she removed them. She says nothing, and I continue to watch her as she pulls oven mitts and takes the pastries from the oven, setting them into the cooling rack. A few more tasks to put everything in order, then she's back standing in front of me, a broad smile on her face.

"Shall we go?"

I nod and like the obedient man I am and follow her out to the parking lot. We walk together to my truck and once she's seated in the cab I walk slowly around the truck and get in. She's back to being silent, and I'm sure at this point she expects me to take her home with me, even though she doesn't actually say the words. It's in the expectation I can feel every time I look in her eyes and in the hope that shines there too; that silent nudge to attempt to get me to allow her deeper into my life, my heart.

But as I pull out of the parking lot, I head toward her condo; my inability to share the space that was once Faith's largely overpowering any need I might have for Emma to truly share that part of my life. I'm positive, with some time and plenty of overthinking on my part, I'll eventually feel comfortable adding memories of her to those of Faith in that space that holds those precious memories of what once was. For now, this will—hopefully---have to be enough.

+++++++++++++++++++++

We spend the majority of the night tearing up the sheets of her big bed. We say very little, unless it's sex related; the 'after' talk replaced by snippets of sleep. Then we eventually pull the covers up and fall together into an exhaustive slumber; Emma curled up against my chest and my arm secured tightly around her.

When I open my eyes in the morning she's gone. The clock tells me that it's almost noon and as I struggle to my feet I realize she may not be the only one feeling the effects of what we've done....muscles I didn't know I had twinge as I move about the room trying to locate my clothes. Dragging on my jeans, I dig around for my cell; see a text from her that was sent very early this morning.

"At the café. Be home by noon. Wait for me." Like I have any other choice, I think to myself. She's obviously taken my truck on her early morning jaunt.

I'm a little thrown by the coldness in the message, then realize I'm probably overreacting. Chances are she's as physically and mentally exhausted as I am. Pulling on my shirt, I head downstairs, past the spare room and extra bath; both simply decorated and spotlessly clean. I head through the living room that boasts an overstuffed couch and loveseat combo and widescreen T.V. and head into the kitchen in search of coffee.

The bright room is simple; painted a soft yellow with white tiles on the counters and floors. Her elaborate coffee machine sits in one corner, and one look at it and I've decided that caffeine is probably overrated. I settle instead on a glass of orange juice and while I sip from it I wander through her space.

As with the upstairs, the décor is simple, understated and elegant; non-descript leather furniture with a few dark, wood tables set around the room for accent. A few black and white photos line the walls; pictures of what I assume are her grandparents, parents and the brother she talks about so often. There are a few other pictures around the room, my favorite being one of Emma as a young child of maybe five or six; the mass of dark hair pulled into pigtails...an oversized apron looped around her neck. I can't help but grin at the wide smile, the sparkling big eyes; this photo the beginning of a career she probably only imagined at that young age.

I'm flipping through the channels when she walks through the door and our eyes immediately lock and hold. Then I'm on my feet, wrapping her in my arms tightly, like it's been days since I've seen her instead of the hours that it actually is. Her small hands grip my back and her entire body melts against mine with what I assume is relief.

"Did you think I'd be gone?" I whisper into her hair.

She shrugs. "I wasn't sure. Everything was so....different with us last night."

What I'm sure she wants to say is that it was cold...everything about last night was cold. From that first frantic joining in the café to the repeated, never ending fucking when we walked through her door, we both seemed driven to inflict pain. And while I have zero complaints about what we did together, I can guarantee that she's rattled by how rough I was with her each and every time.

"Are you okay?"

She pulls back slightly and looks at directly me. "I am. I'm just a little thrown, that's all. I don't usually act like that."

"Neither do I," I reply. Although my one-nighters have gotten pretty crazy in the past, and I've been known to have a major case of the 'what-the-hells' a time or two, I've sure as hell never been out of control when

I'm with a woman. For all the insane times I had with Faith, we never had icy cold, mind-blowing, wall banging, scream inducing, bruising, nail scratching sex like Emma and I had.

"Grace is covering for me. So we can spend the afternoon together." I feel her uncertainty center in my gut. "I hope that's okay."

I hate that I'm the cause of her insecurities; hate that only a few weeks ago she was so self-assured and confident about everything. My disgust with myself, from all that happened last night, to how I've managed to make her feel about herself, sickens me to the core. "Of course it's okay." Leaning down, I brush my lips against hers. There's no more anger, no more coldness, just the warmth between us that we've always had mixed with a heavy dose of doubt.

"So," I begin when I end the kiss and press my forehead against hers. "What do you feel like doing today?"

She smiles. "Doesn't matter to me."

I think for a minute. "Well, we can start with lunch."

"That sounds great. I'm starving."

Pulling out of her embrace, I extract my keys. "I'll head home to shower and change and come back to pick you up. Then we can stop by the café later and get your car."

"I could always go with you," she suggests.

Fear streaks through me and I attempt to shove it down. "That's okay. My place is a mess and I won't be long." My excuse is lame and I can only hope she sees it for what she thinks it is; a bachelor trying to shield his girl from his filth. The truth isn't necessary; especially when I know that eventually I will feel comfortable with her being in Faith's space.

It's not her space you ass, my subconscious shrieks. *It hasn't been her space for years.*

Uncertainty flickers in her eyes. "Oh, okay. Well I'll just see you in a bit."

I hug her briefly, swipe my lips across hers a few more times, then step toward the door. "Be back soon."

Driving home I realize that the tight hold I'm trying to keep on this situation feels like its splintering me into a thousand pieces. I let myself loose on her last night…am now doing everything in my power to keep her from coming to my apartment….and still she manages to look at me with warm, trusting eyes. I hate that I wonder how short-lived that will be;

when she'll finally see me for what I really am....unsure about everything in my life and not at all hopeful that things will change.

I am gonna try, because for no other reason than she's worth it. Just being given the chance to build something with her is humbling; this amazingly exquisite beauty who could have anyone she set her sights on. For now, she's chosen me. And no matter what I do from this point forward, I need to make sure she doesn't regret doing that.

CHAPTER 11

B y the time May rolls around, Emma and I are officially a couple; or
at least that's what Grace keeps telling me. We're together as much
as possible, though our long hours working definitely put a crimp in any
free time we might want to have. Grace has been great, covering the café
on Sunday afternoons so we can spend long hours together doing stuff
regular people do; go to the movies, walk on the beach, or just spending
the entire day in bed. I spend a few nights during each week at her place
and almost always the entire weekend. She's given me a drawer and all the
space in the spare room closet that I want, and once I was able to fend off
the panic about taking this step of moving some things in, we seemed to
finally settle into a nice routine with one another.

The end of May signals Faith's birthday and I'm saved from any
uncomfortable conversations about it because Emma has plans with her
mom that day. Grace is busy with Ryan, so I spend the day like I usually
do each year; drunk off my ass, thumbing through pictures of our past
and allowing the pain to engulf me completely. I give myself this one day,
this one day to remember what was, what used to be, and the day after I
force it all aside and go right back to the life I've been living for the past
few months.

If Emma notices my distance she doesn't say a word, and I wonder if
Grace has clued her into the dates that seem to signal the resurgence of
our grief twice a year. Somehow, I doubt it. For all Grace's closeness with
Emma, I notice that she, like me, goes out of her way to avoid mentioning
Faith. And Emma, for all her honesty and understanding, stays mum as
well. It's like Faith is the invisible elephant in the room sometimes; I can
tell Emma wants to talk to me about her, but I can also tell she's afraid of
what I might say.

I guess I'm not the only one who finds solace in hiding behind the truth.

Being with Emma and living with her most of the time I've learned quite a lot about her; first and foremost I've learned that she hardly ever sleeps. She is so driven, so set on making her business succeed, that even with Grace's help she sometimes doesn't get home until very late at night; and more than a few times she's snuck out early after barely a few hours of sleep. I worry about her and more than once I've tried to get her to take a full day off; to close the shop for a mental health day or something, but she won't hear of it. She will even stay open on most holidays, telling me that at least her customers can always be assured to get a good cup of coffee, regardless if life in general is stopping around them.

In June Ryan plans another party for Grace; although this one is much smaller and is being held at a swanky restaurant. This one is a surprise, so we are all sworn to secrecy weeks ahead of time and when we arrive I can immediately tell that he has more than a birthday celebration planned.

First off, he's white faced, and a fine sheen of sweat beads along his forehead; it would be laughable if the poor guy didn't look so incredibly miserable. There's a huge bouquet of roses on the table for Grace and he keeps fidgeting in his suit pocket with something. And that's another thing…Ryan never, ever, ever wears a suit. His outfit of choice, regardless of the occasion, is a black t-shirt and jeans. Not only does the guy look like he's gonna pass out, he's clearly uncomfortable and out of his element in his clothes. By the time Grace finally arrives with Dad and Ruth, I'm sure that he is gonna throw up. While the entire thing is amusing, I shove a double shot in his hand for reinforcement.

Grace takes the surprise well; hugs Emma and me, lets Moose smack a long, wet kiss on her cheek and then the waiter serves champagne all around. I glance at Emma, see the happiness shining from her eyes, and squeeze her hand tightly when Ryan stands and attempts to get our attention.

"Thanks everybody for coming," He says. He swallows a few dozen times and I silently pray he doesn't spew in front of this group.

"Babe, are you feeling okay?" Grace asks.

He chuckles and shakes his head. "No. Not really." Then he turns to face her straight on; pulling her to her feet as he looks down into her eyes and says, "Grace, you've changed me, in every way possible. Being with you, although at times it feels like a tornado, is the best thing to ever happen to me." When Grace tries to intercede, he immediately puts a finger over her lips and shakes his head. "No talking." She nods and grins up at him. "I love you Grace. And I'm going to love you for the rest of my life." He reaches into his pocket, pulls out a small box and lowers his tall frame down to one knee. Beside me, Emma squeals and clenches my hand tighter.

Ryan takes a shaky breath, flips open the box and rushes forward, "Please do me the honor of becoming my wife. I'll love you and take care of you always."

My crazy whirlwind of a sister starts crying, and leans up and hugs Ryan to her chest. We all start to laugh when he has to pry her off of him to breathe, and again when she jumps up into his arms, lets him lift her off her feet and kisses him senseless. When he eventually sets her down, all color has returned to his face and he's laughing right along with us.

"Grace," Emma urges, "You need to say yes."

Grace starts to laugh and happy tears race down her face. "Thanks Em." She turns her attention back to Ryan. "Yes, yes, yes. Of course I'll marry you. I love you so much!" He grins and slides the large diamond on her hand, and she immediately throws herself at him again.

The small group moves away, giving the couple a few minutes alone. Moose slaps me on the back and congratulates me, although I'm not really sure why. He hugs Emma, though I'm sure that's because she's a weepy, girly mess.

It's a great evening all around; our small family celebrating amidst great food, an abundance of champagne and a lot of laughter. I allow myself one glass of the bubbly, then stick to water for the remainder of the night; this, my vain attempt to get my drinking under control once again. Emma, on the other hand, drinks glass after glass as she and Grace huddle together and start working on wedding plans. I shoot the shit with the rest of the crew and simultaneously try to shove down the memories that push to the surface once again.

Although we spent hours and hours talking about our future as husband and wife, I never did get the chance to ask Faith to marry me. I'll always regret that; regret that we didn't marry, regret that I didn't at least give her that happy memory to take with her. I'm not sure why I ever hesitated; I think I knew from the first day I met her that we'd be together forever. But I guess there never seemed to be the right time; and then I didn't want her to think I was asking just because she was sick.

Sliding that ring on her cold, pale finger ripped something from my soul that I doubt will ever return. I remember looking down at her still, white face and seeing not the girl I'd loved for so long, but the emptiness that remained. And that ring that I'd thought so much about for so long looked out of place and foreign on the hand of the ghost she'd left behind.

I was eventually able to read my vows aloud; not to her and not while she was living, but at a birthday party in her honor. I stood there in Grace's front yard surrounded by family and friends, and pulled from my pocket the words I'd written long ago. My greatest regret, among the dozen or so that I have, is that she never got to hear the vows that I actually wrote way back when we were first together and cancer wasn't even on our radar. I can only hope that one day when it's my turn to leave this Earth, I'll finally be able to share them with her.

There are times like this, and I'll admit they are few and far between as each year passes, that seem to completely knock the wind out of me. I keep imagining her here; her vivacious laughter filling the room as she takes control of the wedding preparations; as she used to take full control of most anything. I can almost see her....green eyes dancing while she talks a mile a minute, waving her hands around and jotting notes down on a napkin. It's a far cry from the almost silent conversation that Grace is having with Emma; their dark heads bent together as they bounce ideas off one another.

I'd love to share this happy news with her, but the idea of visiting her gravesite makes me sick. I wish I could say that I was one of those people who planned my week around visits to the cemetery. But the truth of the matter is that I've not been there...not once...since that day we laid her in the ground. I don't know if it's my denial talking, or just plain fear, but every time I attempt to go out there I end up drinking myself into a stupor. Dumb really....because nothing will change the fact that she's gone.

God I miss her. I miss her laughter, her crazy antics, the abundant love she had for everyone; but mostly for me. I miss the smell of jasmine in her hair and the way she would sometimes just lay her head on my chest and listen to my heart beat. There are thousands of things to miss about her, but mostly I just find myself being sad about what she's missing out on. Life has gone on, no matter how hard I've tried to stop it. And as each day goes by, I get further and further away from her; further submersed in all the new memories I'm creating.

"You all right man?" Moose inquires.

I nod. "Yeah, I'm good." I've gotten so good at hiding my feelings, the lie rolls all too easily off my tongue. Thankfully, Moose is content with a semi-painful back slap of support that rattles my teeth and sends me reaching for another glass of champagne.

Later that night as we're lying in bed, Emma continues with the running stream of conversation that she's been on since we left the restaurant. Thankfully, she's too buzzed to see that I'm not really listening, not really myself; and that the memories are painfully too vivid tonight. Thankfully, she's buzzed just enough to be handsy and needy, exactly what I want to help drive away the memories that I can't seem to escape from. And I'm relentless with her tonight; pulling one orgasm after another from her body, then willingly letting her suck me off until all we can do is flop down on the mattress into a tangled, sweaty heap. She's instantly asleep on my chest, and I'm left staring up at the ceiling listening to her soft snores, and hating myself for once again letting Faith come between us.

+++++++++++++++++++++

Emma

I'm fairly certain that I'm in love with Liam. He's all I think about, even when the café is booming with business. He's the only thing on my mind when I drive back and forth to work, when I'm rolling out dough or even when I'm visiting with my parents. He and I have settled into a nice, crazy life together and there are days that I wish I could just tell him how I feel; let him inside my heart just enough so he understands how very much he means to me.

He's such an easy guy to be with. He's never grouchy, always happy to see me, and gives me pleasure that I didn't even think was possible. Even months into this relationship, we're still as hot for one another as we were that first time in the café, and there are days when that need is so intense it's rather scary. He has no boundaries where sex is concerned, though I'm sure that's because he's far more schooled in the art of lovemaking than I am.

What he doesn't know is that I'd do anything for him, be anything he wanted me to be. As much as I pride myself on my independence, when Liam is around I'm a quivering mass of desperate need. I'll do whatever he asks, try whatever he suggests, if for no other reason than it brings him pleasure.

But there's a vast difference between pleasure and love, and sometimes when I look at him I have to wonder if he'll ever feel for me what I feel for him. There are times when I still see the shadows cross his face and still feel him disappearing into his memories right before my eyes. He's gotten good at hiding it, but I do see it for it is; he's not yet able or ready to let go of Faith. Sadly, I can't help but wonder if he'll ever be ready to let her go. And there are days – many days really – when I fully believe that the ghost of his first love will always be between us.

I hate that I have negative feelings about Faith; it's just stupid. The woman is gone and yes, she might have been everything to him once but there's bound to be a time when he can let her go; even if only to not allow the memories engulf him like they sometimes do. But I admit that I'm puzzled by this invisible hold she seems to have on him and his inability to find even a small measurement of peace about it all.

I've talked with Grace about it, but as usual she's very closed up about the subject of Faith and Liam. So I finally decided to have a chat with Ryan. Even though our situations are different, I know that Grace's grief over Faith impacted their relationship at the beginning too. Unfortunately, Ryan has learned all about keeping things on the Q.T.; gives me the token 'be patient', and blows me off when I attempt to push for more.

If not for the ghost chasing us around, our relationship would be perfect. Liam is still very unsure about meeting my family and for now I'm not pushing the issue. He did meet Mario, but only because they happened to be in the café at the same time. And even though he tried to hide it, I know he was uncertain and none too happy about the forced introduction.

I don't understand this supposed aversion to family at all. I get that his childhood was upended when his mom walked out, even if he refuses to share any details with me, but his dad is great and Ruth seems very caring, so it's not like he doesn't have a support system in place. And the relationship he has with Grace is one I could only dream of having with Mario. They are like one entity; understanding one another without words and staunchly defending the other without question.

I know it's not because he doesn't care for me; because he proves that to me daily just in the way he treats me. But anytime I mention a family dinner or even getting together for drinks with my parents, that wall of his goes up and we end up arguing about it.

I believe that Ryan is right. I knew going in that Liam was going to be a challenge, what with his trust issues and his belief that he's not entitled to be happy, not to mention the huge pile of guilt he wears solidly on his shoulders. I've tried telling him that he is entitled to be happy; tried telling him so many things, but usually he just changes the subject or starts kissing me, which effectively puts an end to any conversation.

I want with Liam what Grace has with Ryan. I want to live together completely, not this half-on, half-off crap that we've been doing these past months. I want to call him mine; in every way. I do realize it's too early to expect flowers and diamond rings, but I'd like to believe we are moving forward or at least toward that direction. Unfortunately, there are many days when it feels like all I'm doing is treading water. There are many days that I'm certain he'll never really be mine; and that Faith's hold on him threatens to remain there forever.

++++++++++++++++++++

Liam

Once fall arrives, the wedding plans are firmly set in motion and Emma is gladly right in the middle of it all. We get together with Grace and Ryan often, although mostly he and I just watch T.V. while the girls drag out their lists and magazines and spend hours talking, jotting down notes and generally ignoring the two of us. All I've been able to pick-up so far is that it's going to be a spring wedding…probably on the beach… and I'm expected to be a groomsman. Other than that, I mostly stay out of their way.

Emma's business is so good that she's hired a part-time employee to help out on busy days and give her some much needed time off. Grace is still waffling on her decision to come to work full-time, although when she's not at her regular job she's always at the café, so I'm not really sure why she's hesitating.

Emma and I decide to take the long Labor Day weekend and head out of town. It's the first time we'll be on neutral territory together; the first time we'll be spending a solid seventy-two hours together, uninterrupted by work or our friends. At Grace's suggestion, we head up the coast toward Monterey Bay, a seaside community where she and Moose have traveled before during those few years when she and Ryan were working things out. We settle into a boutique hotel located on Cannery Row; our ocean-front suite worth every penny of the high-ticket price I paid for it.

The room boasts a massive four-poster bed, with a fireplace and seating area directly in front of the windows that faces the sparkling blue Pacific Ocean. Emma is giddy; excited to be away from the responsibilities of work for the first time in years, and all too happy to show me her thanks for suggesting we take some time to ourselves. She immediately unzips her dress and lets it pool at her feet; the barely there bra and panty set she's got on warming my blood from the inside out. She's intoxicating, a vision with her mass of curls spilling down her back; that perfectly proportioned body a precise fit for mine.

Within minutes, we're naked and the abundance of throw pillows and the fancy comforter are on the floor with our clothes. I take my time with her; trail my lips from her face to her hot pink toes, then back up again. I do this slowly, repeatedly, until I have her begging with need and writhing under me. Then I slide into her slowly; let her absorb every inch until I'm in deep and the urgent need to move is scratching at my spine.

My lips find hers and the kiss is as slow and tortuous as the foreplay itself; and although she's pulling and tugging and trying to get me to move, I'm drawing out the pleasure and trying to cement the memory of this into her heart. I want this to be perfect for her; for the memory of our first trip together to be one that she reflects on often and smiles about.

I wish I could say why I'm so driven to make this special for her. Maybe it's that I feel I owe her somehow, for all the times I check out inside my own head and wallow in memories. Maybe it's that I want to prove to her that we are more than I'd ever admit to out loud, even though my heart is not easily convinced. Or maybe, it's just my driven internal need to make this time different; make the memories different than anything Faith and I experience together.

When I finally start to move, it's with that same slow, measured pace as my kiss. Gone is the urgency that usually drives me, and I let myself love her gently like she deserves; tormenting her with words and grasping her ass in my hands to pull her as close as possible. Her mass of silky hair is spread out over the white sheet, her face flushed and eyes centered right on mine. Her small hands grip my back, the short nails digging into my flesh as I feel her body began to shake; hear the words of pleasure as she reaches her peak. Her straight, white teeth bite down on her lip to keep from screaming and for a brief minute I almost regret the close confines of the hotel. I should have taken her camping….or somewhere where there are no people. I'd really love to hear her let loose.

I continue to move, thrusting into her and riding out the orgasm with her. Then my body takes over and I begin to slam harder and deeper and faster; the fervent urge to come pooling in my gut. And when my eyes lock on hers once again and she throws her arms over head to grasp one of the bed posters, I finish with a few hard deep thrusts and a low groan of release into her neck.

Life around us may be chaotic and uncertain, but everything between us in bed more than makes up for any deficit, at least in my book it does. And as I lie there semi-propped up, breathing in her sweet scent and listening to the rapid sound of her breathing as it begins to settle, I'm sure that with enough time, all the uncertainties with the two of us will work themselves out.

"That was….um…that was…." She whispers, smiling lazily up at me.

I grin down at her and breathlessly state, "Awesome? Mind blowing? The best sex ever?"

Emma starts to laugh and runs her fingers through my hair. "Yep. All of the above."

"Glad you approve," I reply, leaning down to kiss her once more.

We never leave the room that night, electing to order room service and eat naked by the windows. Once we're stuffed and the dinner tray is gone, she pulls me into the massive bathroom and turns on the water in the large Jacuzzi tub. While it fills, I sit on the tiled edge and let her straddle me; the vision in the mirror of her olive skin draped across mine, the slim line of her back and that perfect ass of hers with my hands splayed across it doing crazy things to my body and mind.

I lift her slightly, then let her slide down on my cock; my greedy eyes locked on our images in the mirror behind us. I watch as she lifts up, glides back down; her unhurried motion driving me to distraction just as I did to her earlier, and somehow I manage to growl out, "God babe, I really need you to fuck me."

She smiles and immediately complies; increasing the pace and giving me exactly what I need. Once again my eyes lock on the mirror; at my fingers digging into her bare flesh, urging her deeper and harder with each stroke. That beautiful mass of hair swings with the motion from our movements, which increase to a frantic pace as she starts to come; biting down hard on my shoulder as I work her higher and feel it roll over her entire body. With a final surge and a low, gasping curse, I empty myself into her completely; that vision of us coming together something I'll not yet soon forget.

When I can eventually pry her from my lap, I lower her gently into the sudsy warm water and crawl in behind her small body, pulling her down against my chest. Our fingers thread together on her stomach and one small foot travels up and down my calf as our bodies relax into the water.

"Can I say something?" she whispers.

"Of course." I'm mildly curious about what she has to say - although my brain is still very much muddied from the orgasm - that I don't consider that she'll say anything more than how great we are together.

She takes in a few deep breaths, and then says softly, "I love you Liam."

The roaring in my ears overshadows the chill that races over my body and the sense of dread that settles in my gut. I've worried about this; have seen all the signs...the long-lingered looks she gives me without saying anything, the almost frantic need to please me in each and every way. That being said, I've not once prepared myself for what I should say in response. Do I love her? I have no idea. I enjoy spending time with her, I like the life that we're making together and the stuff we do in bed is outrageous. But... does that mean I love her? I have no frigging clue. It's not at all like what I experienced with Faith, although to be fair she and I had years and years of friendship to base our relationship on and Emma and I have nothing more than a few months; a few rocky months at best.

"I don't expect you to say anything. I understand that this will be difficult for you. But I can't let another day go by and not tell you how I'm feeling." She finally turns her head to look at me. "It's important to me that you know how much I cherish you."

That old familiar need to bolt is bearing down on me; followed quickly by the need to drown my fears in alcohol. It takes a monumental amount of will power, but I somehow manage to shove it all aside and just let her words flow over me. She's right, this is difficult for me; and I'm just arrogant enough to believe that I'd never have to reciprocate any feelings of love or whatever, but just enjoy what she's so willing to give me time and time again. It only further confirms the asshole title I've given to myself, one that I never truly considered that I'd eventually turn on her. But what she doesn't know is that I cherish her just as much. She's made my life whole, for the first time in a long time; and somehow she's managed to - mostly - quiet the voices that are constantly barking at me to hang onto Faith.

"Liam? Are you all right?"

My eyes find hers. "I am. I'm a little thrown, but I want you to know that I cherish you too. And I'm so grateful for what we have together." I have no idea if my words will help or hurt, but it's all I can get out without sounding like a tool.

She turns around and leans against my chest once again. "Do you ever think you might be able to love me too?"

Christ, her words are like a knife in my chest; the desperate plea so out of character for her and proving to me how much damage I'm capable of where she's concerned. "I hope so Em. I really hope so."

She nods and even though I can't see her face I can tell by the shudder that goes through her body that she's tearing up. "Okay."

I'm certain it's anything but okay, however I'm not going to lie to her just to make her feel better. I've only ever loved Faith, and that came so slowly over so many years that I never once felt like I was falling into it. It was more like an acceptance than anything, and sure as hell not this runaway train that Em and I have been on for the past six months.

I'm not sure I know how to love anymore. I am completely sure that the idea of doing so terrifies me. I'd loved once and lost in the worst way possible. Taking a chance on that is not something I think I have the strength or courage to do again. Not even for Emma.

++++++++++++++++++++

Luckily, our little bath conversation doesn't put a damper on the entire weekend. We somehow manage to shrug off the awkward love talk and end up really enjoying our trip. Sunday we spend walking around Cannery Row and after lunch we rent bicycles and ride along the coast toward Pacific Grove; stopping occasionally to take pictures or just watch the sea otters play in the waves. We eat dinner at a seafood place down the street from our hotel, then stroll along hand in hand in the cool, foggy air.

When we return to the hotel I turn on the gas in the fireplace and turn off all the lights; strip her clothes slowly from her body and lay her down on the large bed. I love her silently, with my body, the only way that I know how, until she's panting and sweating beneath me and we're coming together once again.

We sleep very little that night and by late morning we're awakened by the alarm that she somehow managed to set between bouts of lovemaking. I wake her with my lips on her skin; kissing her neck, her chest, drawing a pebbled nipple into my mouth. Drowsily she reaches for me and spreads her legs in invitation, inviting me in to her warm wet body.

Her orgasm is a long slow roll, while mine surges through me hot and fierce until I'm moaning, "Ah..fuck!" into her ear and wondering if this can possibly get any better. When I eventually roll off her and pull her against my chest, spooning her small body into mine, she starts to laugh softly when she wiggles her hips against me and my body instantly reacts.

"God Liam, you are so horny," she says.

"Um…not gonna apologize for it Em."

She laughs again. "Oh, I don't want an apology." She reaches between our bodies and strokes my still semi-hard cock. Then her hips move slowly, a clear indication that she's no more satisfied than I am. When my hand snakes around to rub circles over her hot bud, she moans softly and moves her hips just so; giving me the perfect position to slide right back in.

"Christ…I can't get enough of you," I whisper into her hair.

Her hand reaches back, grips my hip as I increase the pace and she sighs out, "Ah…that feels so good."

I bring her to a quick, hard orgasm and when she's moaning that she can't possibly go again, I roll her onto her hands and knees, grip her hips and start thrusting deeply into her. She's swearing at me…begging me not to stop, then panting out that she can't take it anymore; as much of a contradiction as we are together.

My fingers snake around between legs, resume the caresses that I know will drive her wild. She starts moaning again, calling out for me to fuck her; her words uncharacteristic for her and a testament to how far gone she really is. And it's all the encouragement I need to bring her over once more; let her finally scream out her release into the pillow. I come hard, tightly gripping her hips and growling out her name through clenched teeth.

Once my breathing starts to settle, I pull out and crash down onto the mattress; spooning her once more to my slick body. "Em, you all right?"

She nods, her words clipped and breathless "Uh…yeah. I think so." Her fingers reach for mine. "What are you chasing Liam?"

"Huh?"

Emma rolls over, facing me directly. "What are you chasing? You seem like you're hell bent on proving something. Just not sure it's me you're trying to prove it to."

I really hate that she sees so far into my head, and the denial is on my tongue before I can call it back. "I'm not trying to prove anything, except that we can't get enough of one another."

"Yeah, that's true," she replies, fingers playing with the few hairs on my chest. "But it feels different."

Frowning, I ask, "What feels different? The sex?"

She shrugs. "Yeah, I guess."

"Didn't hear you complaining." I know I sound like an ass, which I am, but I can't help but be defensive. It's my go-to reaction when people push me to places that make me uncomfortable.

Her hands drop from my chest and she rolls onto her back. "I'm not complaining Liam. Not at all. I'm just wondering where all this is coming from."

"All what?"

Her small hands wave around in the air. "All…this. I know you say it's because you can't get enough of me, but I can't help but wonder if it's something else."

"Like what?" I have no idea where she's going with all this, but if I had to guess I'd say her bathtub declaration plays a large part in it.

Her voice is whisper-soft when she speaks. "Like maybe you're running from memories of your past, and keeping your head occupied by fucking me is a good way to hide from the truth."

I'm instantly pissed; the surge of white hot anger igniting my blood. "And what truth is that exactly?"

Emma pulls herself up to sitting; wraps her arms around her knees protectively. "That you're still not over her."

"Fucking Christ!" I snap, rolling upright, my back to her. "Just let it go will ya." In all our months together, I've never once raised my voice to her, so the silence behind me is not surprising. I am surprised by the tears I see when I finally turn around to look at her; streaming down her face and making her appear so small and broken. Guilt slams into me for what I've done; my cold words, my assholish behavior toward her. Immediately I react on instinct; reaching for her and pulling her into my arms, while she starts to sob against my chest.

"I don't know what to think!" she somehow manages between the tears. "I tell you I love you....I know I shouldn't have....and then you're making love to me over and over again...and yet I feel so far apart from you!"

What do I say to her? Do I lie...tell her that I love her just so she'll stop hurting? Do I spew out a bunch of crap, which is guaranteed to just confuse her further? I'm torn between wanting to make things right and not wanting to break her any more than I already have, so I settle on murmuring, "Please don't cry Em."

"I'm sorry Liam," she sobs out, although I have no idea why she feels she needs to apologize. The only person needing to apologize – for everything that's happened this weekend and beyond - is me.

In the end, her tears eventually dry, the deep relationship talk has halted, but the damage has already been done. I'm sure that's my fault; I should quit being so fucking defensive and just tell the girl what I'm thinking, what I'm feeling; even if what I'm feeling isn't something she wants to hear. But something continues to hold me back, keep the truth in, and I can only attribute that to the fear that engulfs me daily; that if I do or say anything wrong I'll lose her for good too.

Our trip home is in relative silence; far different from our trip up North where we took our time and drove along the coast with the music up loud. I take the quick way home; jump on the freeway and go eighty, those worries of mine nipping at my heels like always. She just sits next to me, a tiny shattered version of the smiling, laughing girl that I spent all weekend with; staring out the window avoiding any contact with me unless it's absolutely necessary.

By the time we pull up in her driveway, I'm more than ready to put some distance between us and I'm certain she wants that too. After helping her inside the condo with her bags, I press a quick kiss to her forehead and head for the door.

I've almost escaped when she speaks shakily, fear evident in her voice. "Liam...wait!" She comes toward me, linking our hands together. "Please don't leave."

God my head's a mess! I have no idea which way is up, or what she's gonna say next, and I'm having to force myself to let her guide the way. One minute we're tearing each other's clothes off and the next we're not speaking. It's fucking unpredictable and I realize once again that all I want to do is run; I've wanted that since the moment in the bathroom when she opened her mouth and changed all the rules. Running is easy; too easy.

Staying put is a challenge; one I'm not quite certain I'm strong enough to face. "You sure about that Em? Don't you need a break from me?"

She shakes her dark head. "No. I want you to stay, if that's what you want."

I nod, hope it's convincing enough, and pull her into my arms. Truthfully, I don't really want to stay, but I owe it to her to try. "Yeah babe, it's what I want."

About the only thing I am sure of is my need to be close to her, even though that voice in my head sometimes says differently. Being around Emma does bring me some peace, as long as we're not delving too far into the relationship stuff. And I do know that I sure as hell don't want her here alone, imagining all kids of terrible things.

Or…God forbid…imagining the truth.

What I'm not sure of is the reason for her mini melt-down at the hotel; other than to assume she's harboring some deep resentment because I didn't return her endearment. Maybe I did push hard sexually, but I truly believed she wanted everything just as much or more than I did.

Later that night when we're huddled together under the covers in her bed, I have to force myself to just hold her; keep it simple between us and let her fall asleep in my arms. So when she reaches for me, asks me to make love to her, I'm hesitant; very hesitant.

This time, I'm fairly certain she's the one doing the chasing.

CHAPTER 12

E ach day that draws closer to the October anniversary I find myself becoming more detached from everything; Emma, my family....life in general. This has happened before, so I'm not exactly surprised. It's literally like the month can change from September to October and the thick veil of grief descends over me; my thoughts become consumed by images of Faith, sick and helpless, forcing herself to make future plans that we both know would never reach fruition. It's something I seem to have no control over, and yet I notice I go all too willingly into that black space; letting it swallow me whole and take me in completely into its warm embrace.

It's probably just in my head, I think to myself. I'm more than likely overreacting; anticipating the date for no good reason, other than that it's this sick obsession I seem to have with never letting anything go. It really doesn't matter if it's been five years or twenty; Faith is still gone and she still died a painful, tragic death.

A lot of images have faded over time, but the images of her at her worst....bald, screaming out in pain, begging for me to help her....will never, ever escape my memory. Those images are what haunt me most; in my dreams, in my waking hours, when I'm at work or with Emma. Those are what I can't escape from, can't run from, can't hide from or drink away. They are there constantly, eating away at my gut; the pain as raw and tormenting as when I was actually going through it with her.

"Make it go away Liam....please make it go away....I can't do this anymore." Her voice is broken, barely audible.

"I'm here babe...I'm right here." My words are as empty as the promises that we've received from the doctors.

"Liam...please help me!" Her gasping breath reaches out to me since her hands no longer can.

The nurse gives her another dose of morphine and thankfully she slides into a blissful sleep. And it's then…and only then….do I lay my head down on her hospital bed and cry for this broken girl.

Bile pools in my throat as I recall the memory of that day; one of many in the hospital that would end with us eventually bringing her home to spend her last days surrounded by family and friends and the things she loved best; her beloved music, her favorite stuffed animal, and all the pictures of us together.

My eyes travel to my phone as it blasts from its spot on the counter; the never-ending texts from Emma wondering where I am. I can't face her now, this evening before the day that changed me forever. So I pull up her message, hit reply, and send her some lame message about having a bad case of the stomach flu.

That night I don't sleep at all…I can't sleep….because every time I close my eyes I hear her; pleading with me to take away the pain, begging me to help her even though there's no way I can. Then there are the other memories…memories of conversations we had and things we talked about and promised one another….every one painful and excruciating in its own right.

"Please Liam, promise me." Her voice is barely audible and just getting these few words out is exhausting for her. "Promise that you won't forget me."

I stroke my hand across her soft head; look down into the face I know as well as my own. It's a changed face now; skeletal thin and an odd shade of grey. "I won't forget you Faith. I could never forget you."

By mid-morning I'm blurry eyed and fidgety from too much coffee, the voices speaking clearly to me now on an endless cycle of pain.

"Promise you'll always be my friend, no matter how mad you get?" Sixteen year old Faith stares up at me; green eyes wide with expectation.

"I'll always be your friend." I'm hardly paying attention to her as I finish packing my bags for college.

"Will you call me?"

I glance over at her; fairly shocked to see this vulnerable side to the girl I've always known as a force to be reckoned with. "Yeah. I'll call." Feigning indifference is what I have to do; what I'm forced to do until she's legal and I can make my move….make her mine.

"Don't let those college girls hurt you, okay?"

I ruffle her hair. "They won't kiddo." I give her a knowing smirk. "They will be the only ones getting hurt."

She rolls her eyes at me. "Geez Liam, you can be such an ass sometimes."

My empty stomach rolls as the memory fades away and is immediately replaced by another. All the boxes are out of the closet, the hundreds of photos contained within them scattered on top of the coffee table and spilling out onto the floor; each picture representing a space in time when she was here, full of life and driving me ape shit crazy.

"Geez Liam, what the hell did you just do?"

I grin at her. "I kissed you Faith. You can't be that naïve."

"But why?"

Howling with laughter, I pull her up against my body. "Because I've wanted to kiss you for years now, that's why." I lean down and kiss her briefly once more. "There's plenty more where that came from."

I barely make it to the bathroom before I hurl up all the cups of coffee I've ingested. Once I can successfully get to my feet, I brush my teeth and head back into the living room on shaky, uneven legs. I find it rather ironic that nothing ever changes; neither the memories nor the ability for them to tear me up from the inside out.

The last box of pictures that I've yet to open is from our final year together; snap shot images of her demise right before my eyes. My beautiful girl slowly faded from the energetic red-head I'd loved all my life, to a tiny, hollow, empty version of herself. She never once asked us not to document her life; and even said that we should go back and laugh at how silly she looked without hair or eyebrows.

I've done lots of things the one or two times I've actually looked at those pictures….drank too much, cried for what feels like forever… screamed and yelled and thrown things, but not once have I ever laughed at her emaciated reflection.

Taking out a stack from the top, I flip through them one at time; images of us together at the beach, birthday shots of one of the many years she celebrated with Grace. In some of them she's just her same beautiful self; vivacious and full of life. In others I can see how the cancer started to take its toll; the deep, dark circles under her eyes and the greyish-white pallor that her skin seemed to take on as she got further and further into her treatments. There are pictures of Faith with her parents…with my dad and Ruth….these color images showing the proof that she was fully ingrained in our lives; from way back into our childhood and beyond.

I come to one of just me; I'm smiling happily into the camera, which means that she was on the other side taking the photo. I flip the picture over, looking for a date it was taken, and her perfect script greets me, the words, *"I will love this man for the rest of my life."*

I'm knocked off center; the breath ripped from my lungs so forcefully I can no longer inhale or exhale. Thank God I'm already seated; otherwise I'd be completely knocked off my feet. Tears fill my eyes and I start to shake as I read the words over and over again; words I've never seen before. I've always been so hell-bent on either avoiding the pictures altogether or just looking at them quickly, I never thought to actually turn any of them over.

Like a crazy man, I take another large stack out of the box; turn each photo over and frantically look for any words she might have written to me. Most are blank, or are scribbled with a date only. But as I dig deeper into the box I notice more words written on the back of at least a dozen prints; hear her voice in my head, as clear as if she were right in the room with me now, speaking to me directly.

"I'm not going to be one of those people who leave sad video tapes or letters or shit like that," she says after we drive home from one of the many chemo treatments.

"Babe, don't talk about that stuff." Silence is so much better than hearing that she thinks she's going to die. So far, I've assumed it was just me who saw the writing on the wall; that she wasn't getting better and there would be a time I'd have to say goodbye.

"I'm serious Liam. I might leave you something, but I'm not spending my last days staring into a video camera and telling you how I feel." She reaches for my hand across the cab of the truck. *"I'm gonna tell you that stuff now, so you can hear me say it, see my face and know that they're not just words I've left behind like some consolation prize."*

I stare down at the stack I've uncovered; these tangible messages the final – and only - part of her that I have left to hold onto. I set them aside and go through all the other boxes before I shove everything into a big pile and sit back on the couch with the small stack of messages in my hand.

The first photo is one of us as kids; me, her and Grace that first summer that we met. The girls are in bikinis, although their pre-teen bodies could never really fill them out. I'm next to Grace; my tall, thin frame still underdeveloped and lacking muscle. We're all wet, having just run through the sprinklers; our only real way to cool off in the summertime.

Turning it over, I feel the punch in my gut as I read, *"I knew I loved you even then."* The next picture is of the two of us when we were first together as a couple, at a rock concert for our favorite band. The words read, *"Listen to music Liam. Lyrics will help you heal."*

"Fuck," I growl, hating her for doing this to me; loving her for taking the time to know what I'd need most.

The next one I come to is of me and Grace, all dolled up to go to a wedding or something. *"Let Grace comfort you Liam. Open your arms and let her in."*

I throw the pictures onto the cushion, swipe the tears from my face and get to my feet. Like a crazy man I start throwing open cupboard doors and dragging shit out onto the counter; searching for the bottles I'm sure that I've kept for "emergencies". I'm neck deep in the cupboard next to the sink when my doorbell peels; it's loud, scratchy blast echoing through the small apartment.

Swearing under my breath, I stomp to the door; fully prepared to tell my sister to go fuck herself. Yanking the door open, I'm shocked to see Emma on the other side, and none too kindly snap, "What are you doing here?"

She frowns and pushes at the door with one hand. "I came by to check on you and bring you some soup for when you are able to eat." Her eyes rake me up and down. "Are you okay Liam? You look terrible."

I don't answer, can't answer actually. I'm literally speechless that she's standing at my doorway; this beautiful vision of my future tossed right into the middle of my hellish past.

Emma gives the door another push and strides inside like she owns the place, even though we're both well aware that she's never once been here in all the months we've been together. I watch as her eyes lock onto the disaster I've created in the kitchen; cupboard doors all thrown open and crap spilling out of them onto the counters and floor. She sets the container of soup on a lone bare spot on the cluttered counter then moves slowly back into the living room, where I'm still standing like a statue. Her brown eyes scan the coffee table, the floor and couch, which are littered with hundreds of pictures of Faith.

Bending over, she takes one off the top, then turns to look at me with wide, uncertain eyes. "You're not sick, are you?"

I have no idea what to say to her. The truth will be devastating, but I can already see the wheels in her head going there; watching us slowly start to slip away amidst the wreckage I've tossed on every available surface.

"No," I reply, finally shutting the front door and leaning against it. I am sick, but not in the way she means.

"So that's what this has been about?" The color slides from her face and her eyes grow hard and unfeeling. "That's why you've been so off the past few weeks, because of her?" I don't answer this time; couldn't even if I wanted to. The truth is screaming down at me, at her, and I almost instinctively cover my ears against it. "Tell me Liam! Is that the reason you lied to me about being sick?" I'm stoic, guarding myself against the onslaught and feeling like it's more than deserved.

Emma moves closer to me, the anger and resentment rolling off of her slim shoulders. "How could you lie to me? I've only ever wanted you to tell me the truth. Is that too much to ask?"

When I remain silent, she curses and once more turns her attention to the picture in her hand. It's one of Faith toward the end; her thin figure curled up against me in the hospital bed at her parent's house. Emma spends a good long, few minutes staring at the reflections, and when she finally looks back up at me I'm not surprised to see tears pouring down her face.

"I would have understood if you would have just talked to me about her. Maybe shown me some of these pictures." She tosses the photo down onto the large stack on the coffee table. "But you didn't talk to me about her, did you Liam? You just hid things and lied and made excuses?" She glances around the apartment, then turns back to me shaking her head. "I'm such an idiot. Of course you didn't want me here. I might taint sacred ground for Christ sake." Emma wipes the tears off her face, although it does no good because they are running faster and thicker which each word she utters. "This is the reason you never wanted to meet my family, isn't it?" Once again, I'm silent; the truth roaring loudly in the cluttered room. Might as well let her come to her own conclusions and get it over with.

She swears under breath and moves back into the kitchen, leaning over and resting her elbows on the counter. I'm still silent, coward that I am, and hate that I wish she'd just leave. But I know that I have to allow this time to process, even if I'm the only one who knows the final outcome.

When she eventually turns to face me, her face is flushed with anger. "I would have given you anything! I would have been anything...done anything....given you whatever you wanted or needed. I love you just that much." Her steps toward me are slow and measured. "I wanted a lifetime with you Liam! And I was willing to give you time...give you space...give you whatever you needed to grieve her like you need to. But not once in all the months we've been together have you ever told me the truth!"

She pauses only long enough to catch her breath, then moves closer to where I'm standing, screaming out, "Talk to me dammit! Say something! Tell me that I'm wrong…or tell me I'm right…but man the fuck up. Just say something!"

Our eyes meet and hold; and although I see a whole lot of hatred in hers, the love is shimmering right there too. I have no idea what she sees in mine, but my silence might as well be that final nail in the coffin. I see her fade right before my eyes; the hope, expectation and faith she once had in me all gone in a matter of seconds.

Slowly, I step aside and pull the door open; silently count the minutes until she's gone and I can go back to hiding and running from the truth. Her eyes are filled with tears and when she attempts to reach for me I move away; giving her that one final shove that I know she needs to walk away for good. She might be in pain now, but the chance of her having a beautiful future is once more attainable with me finally out of the way.

"Please don't do this Liam. Please fight for us. Fight for me." My unending silence is her answer and as she moves past me she whispers, "I wish I'd been enough for you."

I slam and lock the door behind her and immediately return to the kitchen. I can't think about her now. If I do, I'll never survive. What I did is for the best. What I did she will eventually thank me for. I'm not a whole person – I may never be – and I'm simply not able to give myself to someone the way I should. I doubt that I ever will be able to. Something broke inside of me when I lost Faith, and even Emma…beautiful, amazing, generous Emma…could not bring me back from the dark abyss that I've been cocooned in for years now.

The bottle of vodka is buried in one of the last cabinets I check; and next to it is a bottle of Jack Daniels. I take out both bottles, head back to the couch and crack open the first bottle.

++++++++++++++++++++++

For the next few weeks I exist on alcohol, work and small snippets of sleep that I eventually fall into in a drunken slumber. I'm hung-over every day at work, plowed out of my mind on the weekends, with only one goal in mind; drink my pain away.

I avoid the phone, the door, the mail that's piling up on the counter. I avoid food, because I'll just eventually puke it up when the alcohol reaches its peak. I'm a frequent customer at my local liquor store; stocking up on numerous bottles every few days and drinking myself senseless each and every night.

Grace has been relentless; blowing up my phone with voicemails and texts, leaving notes on my door when I'm not home. When I am home, I avoid her knock; bolt the door from inside so that she can't use her key. After the first week she stops coming around. She knows me well; she knows I need space before I can even think about working my way back to the living.

But this time is different than all those others times in the past; this time I've lost twice. I have the memories of both girls to torment me now; that, and the mountain of regret that hangs on my shoulders like a five hundred pound weight.

I do eventually read the backs of all the pictures; Faith's haunting words to me no longer the salve they should have been. I blame her for bringing me down so far again; I blame Emma for pulling me into her web and letting me believe I had a chance on a future, on happiness. I blame my sister, for being able to move on with her life while I'm stuck here in nothingness. I blame everyone except myself; so I let the bottle do that for me.

By the third weekend I'm barely conscious of how much I'm drinking. I sit on the couch, surrounded by all the memories, guzzling the Jack like water. I hardly remember opening the second bottle; though I do recall at some point I spent some time in the bathroom, emptying my stomach and preparing it for round two.

Faith's favorite Daughtry song is on repeat, as it's been since my discovery of those picture messages. Like the song claims, she crashed into my life; and at the time I had no idea that years later I'd be physically unable to walk away from her.

The booze slides down smoothly and my already blurry vision gets more distorted. I hear ringing…probably my phone; although I have no idea where it even is. I attempt to get to my feet and immediately plummet to the ground; laughing hysterically as I hit my head on the coffee table but somehow manage not to spill any of the liquid out of the bottle.

I reward my finesse with another large gulp.

Propping myself up against the couch, I pick-up one of the pictures; my favorite one of Faith and I together. Grace took it, one day when we were all just hanging out at the beach. The sunset was behind us and she's wrapped in my arms; the love between us so evident just by the looks on our faces.

Turning it over, I read the words she left me. *"Please love again. I can't bear the thought of you being alone. I want you happy Liam, don't forget that."*

I hurl the empty Jack bottle across the room, where it shatters against the wall. Fucking Faith, how the hell could she do this to me? She said she would tell me everything while she was alive, then she goes ahead and leaves me this shit. What the fuck am I supposed to do now?

I toss back the now opened vodka and begin to drink it down like water; feel myself start to slip into that fuzzy, happy place where I much prefer to be. My last conscious thought is that I hope Emma never has to see me like this. I hope she can forget about me, go on with her life and be happy.

+++++++++++++++++++++

I hear beeping.
Relentless, obnoxious beeping.
Beep….beep…..beep…..
There are voices too, but I'm too far gone to make them out.
Beep….beep….beep….
"Blood pressure….."
Beep….beep…..beep…..
"Breathing is labored."
Beep….beep…..beep…..
Faith? Are you here? Faith!
Beep….beep…..beep…..
I can feel hands on me….something shoved down my throat….the feeling like I need to puke but can't. I'm poked…pushed at….turned on my side….Emma? Are you there?
Beep….beep…..beep…..
Then I'm sliding….back into my heavenly, dark abyss; greeted by my green eyed angel who waits for me with open arms.

+++++++++++++++++++++

My first conscious thought is that I hurt. My entire body aches, like I've been beaten or run over or dropped face first off a cliff. Even just a small wiggle of my toes sends pain shooting through my body, though that one movement does pull me fully awake and somehow forces my eyelids open.

I'm once again in a sterile hospital room, though this time I'm all alone. The relentless beeping has stopped, but I notice I'm hooked up to at least five different IV bags and the rails on my bed are up to prevent me from falling out of bed.

My small attempt to turn my head sends another shot of hot searing pain slicing through my body, so I settle instead on just rolling my eyes around; which is less painful but still leaves me breathless all the same. I'm in a small private room with a window that has bars across it. There's a small sink, a door which I assume leads to a bathroom and a miniature closet. A crappy old T.V. hangs from the ceiling and I have my doubts whether or not it actually works or even gets more than one channel.

I hear voices outside my door and when I can manage a slight turn of my head I can see the back of Grace's head through the glass. I can't hear what's being said, can only see her dark head bob up and down in agreement. I see her glance into my room, her eyes widen when she sees me looking at her, and a minute later she's coming through the door.

"How are you feeling?" she asks as she makes her way to me.

"Crappy," I whisper. Talking hurts too apparently. My throat feels like someone took a knife to it.

Grace's eyes fill with tears. "Fucking hell Liam, do you have any idea how scared I was, finding you like that?"

I have no idea what she's talking about; my foggy memory sketchy at best. "Um...no?"

She throws up her hands, curses again and walks toward the window. "I found you passed out in your apartment. You were practically drowning in your own vomit and barely alive."

I hate that I wish she wouldn't have found me, but the truth is all too real. Living is painful; death is way too easy.

Grace turns to face me, her face white, blue eyes hard with anger. "You asshole. I'm so sick and tired of your fucking self-pity and thinking you're the only one who has ever been in pain." She takes two steps toward me. "I loved her too God dammit! And you don't see me ending up in the hospital...twice....because of it."

She runs her hands through her hair, swipes at the tears on her face and resumes her spot next to me. "This is over Liam. Enough already. Faith is gone. She is dead, do you hear me? Say the words and fucking believe them. She's dead…she's never coming back…and you need to move on with your life."

She's right…about everything. I know and I even believe it now, which is a shocker. It's just the letting go part that I seem to have issues with. Throw in all the shit with Emma, my beautiful brown-eyed girl who I just tossed aside like she never even mattered, and I'm a hot mess of regret and agony.

"You need help big brother. Help I can't give you. I've tried…Emma has tried and you're just unreachable." Her hand snakes out and drags through my hair. "Please get yourself some help Liam. Do it for Faith… for Emma…for me…for yourself. I don't care who you do it for but please, please, get some help."

She's sobbing now and I realize that I've finally managed to break her too; this amazing girl who has always stood right by my side and fought for me every step of the way. "Gracie, come here." I pat the side of the bed, feel the pain shoot up my arm.

She lowers the bedside rail and gently climbs in next to me; sobbing against my chest as I pull her in tight, although it takes super-human effort on my part because the pain is quite literally taking my breath away. It's just the ass kick I need; that, and this shattered girl crying in my arms, to wake me and for the first time pull the blinders off.

Grace is right. I do need help. I hate the idea of unloading my shit onto some stranger, but I also know that if I continue to attempt to work through all this on my own, I'm going to turn into a raging alcoholic. If I'm honest with myself, I probably already am one; I've just been really good at hiding it from everyone, including myself.

The truth is that alcohol isn't my solution; it never has been. It's been a way to escape, a way to hide from the truth, hide from pain….hide from my life. I've slowly let myself fall into that dark place I could never believe I could go. And the scary thing is, I went there so easily; too easily actually. I willingly allowed my memories to alter the direction of my life and have full control over my decisions.

Getting help won't be fun. In fact, the idea that I'm going to have to relive everything….again….is enough to make me want to take another drink. But, I want to stop hurting people more than I want that drink. I want to stop hurting….period.

"I love you Liam. So much."

"I love you too Gracie."

CHAPTER 13

I wake to the sound of raindrops on the skylight above my head; the gentle pitter patter softly cascading down onto the glass. Propping myself up against the pillows, I gaze around the room.

Boxes are piled in the corner, pictures propped up against the wall, reminding me that I have a busy day ahead of me. I just moved into this new place yesterday, a condo that Grace found for me while I was in rehab. She even packed up all my shit from the other place, cleaned it out thoroughly, so that I never had to return to the apartment that once held so many memories - good and bad - and so very many mistakes.

Throwing off the covers, I get to my feet and drag on yesterday's clothes. I'll look for clean ones later, once I figure out which box Grace packed them in.

Heading down the short flight of stairs more boxes greet me in the small living room and my furniture is just stacked in one corner; leaving the room design up to me.

I notice that lots of things are being left to me now, which is pretty odd considering that in the last few months most things have been out of my control complete. I've been told when to wake up, where to go, what to do and pretty much have had zero control over my life.

After my three days in the hospital, where I was poked and prodded and eventually pronounced healthy enough to leave, I went to stay with my dad and Ruth. As a family we attempted to work together to try to tackle my demons, and once I tried to see a therapist. But when the pull of the bottle started to draw me in once again, I realized I needed more help than my family alone could provide.

So I started making calls, inquiries….and after a full assessment I was put into a 30-day alcohol rehab program. As I had thought it might be, it was one of the most painful things I could have ever gone through. In a lot of ways it was more painful than losing Faith. All my monsters were raised to the surface and there were days….a lot of days actually….when I was convinced I'd just drown in my pain. There were more days that I'd just pray for it all to end; take the easy way out once again instead of facing what I fear the most….admitting to myself that she is really and truly gone.

With therapy…individual, group and family therapy….I eventually started to see the light. I started working my plan, putting those 12 steps into place that I'd always heard about and going to meetings every day. It's been a very slow process, but this move is certainly a step in the right direction.

There are more boxes stacked in the kitchen, but thankfully the one marked "coffeepot" is right on the top. Once I've got a full pot brewing, I switch my phone on and check messages. Surprisingly, there's only one; Moose checking in to see if I need help unpacking. I hit him back, tell him I'm good, and thank him for helping out the day before.

I'm sure I have a lot more to thank him for; his friendship, his support these past months, being there for Grace when she was chasing her own demons a few years ago and I was checked out; hiding from life, as usual. I learned a lot about myself during therapy; a lot of it really ugly stuff actually. I learned how I had perfected the art of hiding; behind the bottle, behind the pain, behind the sex with the one-nighters and Emma too. I learned that I'm a selfish bastard; full of self-pity, self-loathing and that I've mastered the art of being a martyr.

What a shocker.

It would be easy to hate myself after all that I learned, but learning where it all stemmed from helped me to realize how out of control I've been….for years now. I know I've still got a lot of healing to do, but for the first time in a long time I finally feel like both feet are firmly on the ground.

The knock at the door startles me out of my deep over-thinking and I pull it open to find a smiling Grace greeting me on the other side; her arms full of grocery bags. "Morning big brother. Please tell me you have coffee."

I grin at her and reach for one of the bags. "Yep, it's almost done." I follow her into the kitchen. "What's in the bags?"

She shrugs and begins to unload items into the fridge and cupboards. "Just picked you up a few groceries to tide you over for a few days."

"Ah Gracie, you such a good little wife," I tease.

Her eyes roll. "Shut up and pour me some coffee."

We shoot the shit and drink coffee and eat the donuts she knew we'd both need. She gives me the latest wedding plan update, spends a few long minutes bitching about catering costs, and then we get to work unpacking boxes and organizing furniture.

By early afternoon the living room and kitchen are completely unpacked and we're upstairs working on the bedroom. She's made two trips to Target to buy me crap I probably don't need, like new bath towels and three new rugs. I ordered pizza for lunch, and together we consumed the entire thing. And now I'm listening to her grumble on and on about the sad state of my bedding.

"These sheets are a joke," she grumbles, folding my one extra set and stashing them in the hall closet. "I'm getting you some new ones."

"Stop it Grace. You don't need to spend any more of your money on me." My eyes meet hers. "And besides, it's just me now so why do I care what my sheets look like?"

Sadness rolls over her face. "It won't always be that way Liam."

I shrug; way too at peace with the fact that I'm going to be alone for a very, very long time. "Yeah well, at least for the foreseeable future, I don't need to worry about having nice sheets."

She gives me a long hard look. "Yeah, I guess so." We work together for another few minutes before she asks, "Have you heard from Emma?"

Hearing her name sends a wave of pain and regret lacing through my body. "No. But I don't really expect to. We're done." The sad truth is that the kindest thing I could have ever done for Emma was to let her go. And truthfully, I should have done it right at the start; should never have let our infatuation turn into anything more than a hot attraction for one another. I still miss her; miss her sweet laughter, that beautiful smile, the gentleness she wore so naturally. I'm quite certain I'll always miss her. Emma was my one chance at real happiness, and because of my choices I hurt her in ways that are unforgivable. I can only hope she can manage to eventually move on and find love and happiness she deserves.

I glance across the room at Grace, see her watching me as I war with myself internally. "How is she?"

Grace blows out a deep breath and gives her head a small shake. "I don't know. She won't talk to me, not really. She tells me that our friendship will suffer if she talks about you." She gnaws on her upper lip and sits on the corner of the bed. "I worry about her Liam. She works all the time and she looks so tired and....so lost."

I nod, fully owning now all that I did to her. "She told me she loved me."

Grace offers up a half-smile. "I'm not surprised. The girl melted whenever you walked in the door."

I scrub my hands through my short hair. "Yeah well, I managed to screw up her life completely so I doubt she loves me anymore."

Grace raises an eyebrow in my direction. "You so sure about that? As you well know, it's not so easy to fall out of love."

Leaning against the wall, I shove my hands in my pockets. "Yeah, that's true." My fingers grasp onto the list, the one I made in rehab and carry with me always; the list of all those I've harmed during the course of my spiral into alcohol. Emma's name is first on that list, though she will probably be the last one I actually make amends with. Facing her, at this point in my recovery, is impossible.

"Stay here. I have something for you," Grace states, running from the room and down the stairs. I hear the sound of the front door opening, and a minute later it's being slammed closed; her feet pounding back up the stairs. She's holding a large flat item, which appears to be a frame, though I can't actually see it because it's wrapped in brown paper. She thrusts it at me and announces, "Housewarming gift."

I tear the paper; tossing the remnants onto the floor. As I predicted, it's a frame; thick and black and heavy. Under the glass are the twelve photos that I set aside months ago when my life unraveled right before my eyes. Faith's words are written in perfect scroll under each picture; her gentle reminders to me to live again. The picture in the middle is larger than the others and is of the three of us that first summer; grinning into the camera lens as we consume monster-sized double scoop ice cream cones. The words, *"Never forget to smile"* are written underneath.

"Ah Grace…this is amazing. Thank you." My throat is thick with tears as I take in Faith's words of wisdom and let them heal me from the inside out. I suppose this is why she left them in the first place, only I was too stupid to see the truth in them before. I should have known that Faith would never have done something to hurt me and would have only wanted to find a way to bring me some peace, some closure.

"I thought it was a good way to…you know.…. say goodbye." Her words are carefully chosen, but I know she realizes what I've finally discovered; it's time to let Faith go.

"It's perfect," I reply, setting the frame aside and pulling her into my arms.

I've given myself more than enough time to grieve the loss of Faith, and although I know there will never be a day when I won't miss her, that stabbing sense of pain is finally gone. Talking about it, and about her, has helped. Putting my shit in order has helped more. I'm not foolish enough to think that I won't still have bad days because of her, but the what-ifs seem to be silenced for now.

My therapist told me it wasn't surprising that I turned to alcohol as a crutch; which was mostly likely triggered by Faith's illness and the endless hours and days caring for her. The sense of abandonment from losing my mom too, just added to the negative feelings and inability I had to actually experience real emotion. Alcohol, he informed me, was just a salve for the pain I never allowed myself to feel or express; which is why when I was sober I volleyed between happiness and just being an asshole. My rollercoaster moods have since mellowed out, though I do worry most that I'll fall back into that easy place where denial worked well for most every part of my life.

"Ok, let's get this shit done so you can buy me dinner," Grace says, pulling out of my arms and heading right back to work on my closet.

Grace was the first person I made amends with; an entire night spent reading her the list of ways I've wronged her in the past. As usual, she tried to fight with me over every one, until I eventually had to make her promise to just shut up and listen. Since that time, she's routinely joined me for therapy appointments and we've started talking in depth about things we experienced…good and bad…with Faith.

It's so strange, because for so long her name was like a taboo subject to me; don't mention her and it will somehow mean that she isn't gone…. that was the twisted truth I lived with in my head. But therapy…and being alcohol free…has helped me to see that talking about her changes nothing; she is gone regardless. It does however help those that are left behind; those left with the scars from her sickness, and from her loss.

I still have all the boxes of pictures, tucked away in the garage where they're accessible if I need them. Right now, I'm content to have this one frame; this one visual image of the many years we had together. At the heart of our relationship was the friendship we created, which somewhere along the line I lost focus of. Yes, we loved one another, and yes, we were planning a future together. But my therapist helped me to see that her loss was a much larger picture; future wife, lover, and longtime friend…and when those memories starting flooding my head that's when I split wide open.

I'm so grateful that through it all...through all the awful things I've done...my family has stuck by me. I'm very grateful for the support of Moose and Ryan. I'm thankful that my boss's sister is a recovering alcoholic and he knows exactly what I'm going through. I'll be forever grateful to him for holding my job until I'm mentally able to return.

And...as I've learned over the past few months....I'm so grateful for the two amazing women who have loved me. I have reached a peace about Faith...finally....but I know it will be a long time coming before I feel that same way about Emma. In a way, I have so many more demons where she's concerned. I used her in every way possible; to keep my crazy head busy and to distract me from myself. I used her goodness and light as a reason to behave like a dick to her, and I frequently used her body to escape in. Yes, we had fun together and yes, there were times I did treat her well, but overall I took her for granted and I never once gave her the love and attention she deserved.

Talking about Emma is still very difficult. It's easy to lock up and deny what I've done; deny how I lied to her again and again when she only ever asked me to tell her truth. In the end, my silence probably hurt her more than any nasty words I could have spewed out. My silence told her she didn't matter and that she wasn't worth my time to argue with. I'll regret that most of all; because she matters more than I can possibly ever admit.

+++++++++++++++++++++

"My name is Liam and I'm an alcoholic."

I look out into the group of mismatched people from all walks of life and realize as I do every time I come to a meeting that it's possible for this disease to affect anyone, regardless of race, social status or age.

I've only ever spoken one other time and halfway through my story I totally fell apart and had to leave the podium. I was mortified, sick at myself for succumbing to my fears. But when I realized that there was no judgment, and that more than a few folks had reacted the same way their first time, I started to believe in my ability to walk this walk, one day at a time.

"I started drinking five years ago, after the love of my life died of breast cancer."

Yes, I actually said the words…out loud…without screaming or crying or running. I look at the front row, into those blue eyes that are identical to mine; see the tears and the smile and know without her saying so that she's proud of me.

"I drank to escape the pain, to not feel anything…good or bad. I hurt people…hurt myself…and acted like a complete asshole." My heart is racing in anticipation; palms sweaty, lump in my throat. "And when I eventually got into another relationship I used alcohol and my pain to treat her like crap and to avoid getting close. I hurt her in ways that I can never apologize for." A few tears escape and roll down my face. "But I do want to try. Eventually. Some day." I glance back out at the crowd. "Thanks for listening."

I resume my seat and put my arm around Grace; let her cry silently against my chest while I listen to the next speaker. I'm a big believer… now…in learning from other people's mistakes, so I listen intently each time I come; take internal notes and use the information I gather from others to remind myself that I have a lifetime of healing ahead of me.

After the meeting I take her to lunch at our favorite burger joint; laugh as she rambles on about the wedding plans. The wedding is scheduled for early May; a good new memory for that month, she's told me often, and a new reason to smile instead of feeling sad. Besides, as she likes to remind me, Faith would be elated to have the wedding the same month as her birthday.

"I need to tell you something," Grace says, dipping her fry in ketchup.
"Yeah, okay."

She raises concerned, blue eyes at me. "Emma is my maid of honor."

I smile at her. "I figured. No worries Gracie. It will be fine." Since I had anticipated at least seeing Emma at the wedding, I've been talking at length with my therapist about it and how I should handle things when I see her for the first time since that fated day in my apartment last October.

She gives me the doubt-filled raised eyebrow. "Hmm. You sure about that?"

I nod. "I am. I'll be friendly and I won't bother her. And please tell her that if she brings a date I won't freak out." I have been anticipating this too, although the thought of Emma with someone else is pretty hard for me to swallow, even now.

Grace grins at me. "She'll probably just go with Moose."

I refuse to let her see how relieved I am. "Yeah okay. Well, please tell her anyway."

"Okay." Her eyes find mine again. "So then I should also tell you that I'm quitting my job and going into business with her."

Smiling, I reach for her hand. "Ah Grace, that's great news. I know Em always wanted you there with her. And it will really help her out having you there full time." A wave of sadness rolls over me. I wish I could be a part of all that again…a part of her life, her café… but I know it's an unrealistic expectation on my part. I have no place in her life anymore.

"You miss her don't you?" Grace asks softly.

I'd like to deny it, because that's what I used to do; that's my old "normal" way of coping with anything that made me uncomfortable. But the new me….the 'put everything out there' me….can only tell her the truth. "Yeah, I do. Every single day."

"Talk to her Liam. Tell her what you've been through. She'll understand."

Shaking my head, I throw my napkin on my plate; my appetite now gone. "I can't. Not yet." I'm not about to try to put myself out there when I'm still so unsure about how I feel about her, and when I still have a lot of work and healing left to do.

"Okay," she replies, though I can tell she's less than happy with my decision. My sister is always at her best when she's matchmaking.

I don't tell her, but I'm worried about seeing Emma at the wedding; worried more about her reaction to me than my reaction to her. I'm certain that by the time I actually lay eyes on Emma, I'll be so scared shitless of her seeing me after what I've done, that I'll just stand there and say a whole lot of nothing.

I'm genuinely concerned that she'll do one of two things; lambast me with a list of all the ways I've wronged her, or just flat out ignore me. I've sorted through ways to handle both instances, and still feel sick every time I imagine that look of hate on her face that I know I'm bound to see. Even when I first met her, she still found time to be kind to me, but I'm quite certain I've severed that as well.

Being in a good place mentally at the wedding is my top priority. It's going to be a long few days where I'm forced to spend time with her; forced to put on a happy face for my sister and Ryan and put my own shit on the back burner for now. Working my steps, going to therapy and to work every day will definitely help me be in a good headspace when I see her. I just hope that my heart will follow suit.

++++++++++++++++++++

Emma

I glance at the clock, see that it's after midnight and tell myself that I need to get home and try to get a few hours' sleep. Sleep has been hard to come by these past long months since I walked out of Liam's apartment and left my heart in pieces on his cluttered floor. Since then I've moved in slow motion; going through the day to day duties like normal, refusing to think about the times we were together here in the kitchen, and sleeping on the couch to avoid his smell which still lingers on the sheets and pillows in my bedroom.

His clothes and other things he kept at my place have been boxed up, waiting for him to pick them up or send someone to get them. I've heard nothing. I once asked Grace if I should give the stuff to her, and she just told me she didn't want to get in the middle of us. I tried telling her there is no us anymore, but she likes to ignore me sometimes.

I don't ask her about him, mostly because I promised myself and her that I'd keep my past with Liam a subject we no longer talk about. It's hard sometimes, as I watch her dance around mentioning his name or telling me something; something I'm sure she would tell me…her best friend….if I wasn't still in love with her brother; the man who crushed me completely.

I do talk to Moose about him…a lot. Moose is a great listener and although he refuses to divulge anything too private he did tell me about Liam's hospitalization. Of course, I didn't find out about it until months after the fact; long after I could actually panic when I heard he almost died from drinking too much.

When I asked Moose if Liam got some help for his drinking, he only said yes; so I've tried to come to my own conclusions. I've driven by his apartment once, but the old lady and man sitting on chairs out in front told me that he'd moved out after Thanksgiving. It appears that he changed his life completely without once looking back at me.

It's a very hard pill for me to swallow, knowing how much of myself I was willing to give to him; and how much he deliberately withheld from me. Seeing him in pieces that night, the shattered man surrounded by memories that torment him on a daily basis, made me realize I probably never really knew him at all; only the parts of him that he wanted....or allowed....me to see.

I do believe that he tried with me. I do believe that we had some genuinely happy times together, as evidenced by the pictures that I printed out and have stashed in my sock drawer. I do believe he cared for me, although I have my doubts as to how much. And I do believe he thought he wanted us, at least for a little while.

That's all over now and once I get through the wedding I'll no longer have to see him. I realize our paths may cross due to my friendship with Grace, but I plan on doing everything in my power to avoid us seeing one another in the future. I'm willing to do this for him, so that he can heal and find whatever peace he's looking for. I do it for myself because it's still too excruciating to think about looking at him...loving him...and knowing he feels nothing for me except that I'm a good way to escape what troubles him most.

My mom has asked me about him frequently; asked unending amounts of questions about this man whom she never met. I tell her snippets of information, but I know she can see the depth of my pain; she is after all my mom and knows me better than I probably know myself.

I think about Liam often and wonder if he's back drinking again or if he finally found some control over that craving. I wonder if he ever thinks about me; about the happy times we had at the café, at my condo or just hanging out with our friends. I wonder if he's back to screwing all the random girls; using them to chase away his ghosts like he once used me. The thought makes me physically ill and it's one I try to ignore, but sometimes it gets the better of me. My tears have finally dried and now all I feel is numb...empty...lost.

I wonder if that's how Liam felt after losing Faith. Guess I'll probably never know.

CHAPTER 14

The day before the wedding I take off from work; go to an AA meeting, tell my story, then head to therapy for an extra-long session. My therapist, Paul, walks me through my concerns for the next few days, when I'll be obliged to face Emma over and over. I'm going to be forced to deal with how much I've hurt her; forced to deal with all my fears face to face. But no amount of therapy is ever going to prepare me for what I'm going to see in those beautiful brown eyes of hers. No amount of therapy will ever prepare me for my reaction to just being in the same room as her once again.

I go back to another AA meeting that afternoon before heading home to shower and dress for dinner. Luckily there's not an actual rehearsal, since we're mostly winging the whole thing; at least that's what Grace tells me. Moose is picking me up, electing to be my support system tonight; although he's quick to inform me that he's unavailable the next day. He doesn't say why, until I push him and he confirms that he's Emma's date for the big event.

I plan on spending a lot of time with my dad and Ruth and some of the family friends I haven't seen in a while. My sponsor's number is already on speed dial in my phone; and he's more than anticipating a few frantic calls when things get out of my control in my head, which I readily assume they will the minute I lay eyes on her.

Moose, as usual, yammers a mile a minute while we drive to the restaurant; some local Italian place that my dad has chosen but that I've never been to. I'm a bundle of nerves, convinced that I won't be able to eat, and admittedly jonesing for drink. I pull out my phone, dial my sponsor; let him talk me back into a good place before we pull into the parking lot.

"You all good man?" Moose asks, scrubbing one thick paw across his bald head.

"Yeah. Let's go."

The non-rehearsal dinner is being held in the banquet room in the back of the restaurant and each step I take behind Moose increases my anticipation and fear about seeing Emma. I know I need to do whatever I can to set my own crap aside for once. This night is about Grace and Ryan after all and not my obsession with setting everything right in my world. My shit will have to take a powder for the next few days and once all is said and done I can deal with the aftermath of facing Emma.

We're the last ones to arrive; pretty typical for Moose as he's always running at least ten minutes behind. It's a small group, since Ryan isn't very close with his extended family. His mom is gone and his dad, like me, enjoys the bottle a little too much; although like me he has sought treatment recently and is in attendance tonight. Dad and Ruth are seated at the one long table across from Ryan and Grace; Ryan's dad is next to him and Emma is seated next to Grace.

We greet the group and I let Moose take the lead; his loud booming voice and infectious laughter taking all the attention away from me. He takes the seat next to Ruth and I obediently sit in the chair beside him; the chair that just happens to be directly across from Emma. I've yet to actually make eye contact, but I can feel the tension rolling off her from across the table.

The waiter arrives, rattles off the specials and offers Moose and I some wine. I decline, order a club soda and occupy my vision with the menu. Chatter is going on around me; Grace excitedly talking about their honeymoon trip to Jamaica, Moose chiming in every so often to make some crass joke, then immediately apologizing to Ruth for his rudeness. Both the dads pipe up occasionally and I silently wonder if anyone notices the thick silence circulating around me and Emma. I know that I don't dare look at my sister; I'm sure just one look from her will leave me in shreds on the floor.

Once our orders are placed, my dad gets to his feet and raises his glass. "I'd like to make a toast to Gracie and Ryan. May you always make each other happy and be each other's best friend. Remember to never go to bed angry and to always be truthful with one another, even if you're afraid of the other person being hurt by the truth."

His words stab me in the gut like a knife and my eyes immediately shoot across the table; for the first time in months seeing the brown eyes that haunt me on a minute by minute basis.

She looks beautiful, more than I could have ever imagined, and I can't believe how easily she can stun me with just a look. That amazing mass of wavy hair is shorter now, though it still flows over her shoulders in a silky mass. There are circles under her eyes; deep, dark ones that tell me she's working too hard at the café and not sleeping nearly enough. I wonder idly if she's having trouble sleeping because of me, then shove the thought aside. I'm her past now. I sure as hell have no right wondering what keeps her awake at night.

She looks at me with a blank expression; void of anger or resentment or warmth. It's like there's nothing there; like everything inside her has been yanked out, leaving an empty, exquisite shell. I watch as her eyes trail over me. I wonder if she sees the war I've been through these past months. Then her eyes skirt away, down the table, anywhere but right at me as she raises her glass high in the air and solutes the couple.

Moose casually lays his arms across the back of my chair; gives my shoulder a firm, hard pat of support. I'm sure he witnessed our exchange; certain he knows the inner turmoil I'm going through. He's been with me enough in the past few months to know how Emma can be a trigger for my need to drink.

I somehow manage to make it through the rest of the evening without completely falling apart. I contribute to the conversation when I'm pushed, but mostly I talk with Moose, push my food around my plate, and excuse myself twice to go out to the lobby to call my sponsor. Avoiding the bar is my biggest challenge, and it's just the rude awakening that I need for how much work I still need to do.

Moose and I are the first to head out. Good friend that he is, he gives Grace some lame excuse about a hot date he's meeting later tonight, but I know she sees the truth; that he's getting me out of there before I come completely undone. When we're finally out at the truck, I spend five minutes just leaning against the door, trying to calm my racing heart and settle my uneasy stomach. Then I spend five more minutes talking myself down from heading to the closest liquor store.

"Need a meeting?" Moose asks when I finally settle in the seat next to him.

I hate to admit it, but I do…desperately. "Yeah." I rattle off the address of one that holds late night meetings, and within ten minutes we're walking through the door. The minute I'm seated I finally start to feel calm again; finally feel the scratching need that's been tearing at me start to abate.

"My name is Liam and I'm an alcoholic."

I go through my story, gain strength from my best friend and the folks seated around the room. Then I lean my elbows on the podium and just let the words flow. "I saw her for the first time tonight. And there were two things I immediately wanted. To run and to drink." I scrub my hands over my face. "My therapist tells me it's because being with her makes me feel...makes me feel everything....and I've done nothing but hide and run and drink away my feelings for years now." A bunch of heads nod in the group, a clear indication to me that I'm never alone in my struggle. "I have to see her again tomorrow and as scary as that is I'm more afraid to realize that it could be the last time I ever lay eyes on her." Tears well up and spill over without me even realizing it. "I want to see her again more than I want to drink, and I think that scares me the most." Again, many heads nod in agreement. "Thanks for listening."

I fall into the chair next to Moose, lean over and cover my face with my hands and just let the sadness take me over completely. I'm still sitting like that when the meeting is over; when my anonymous family members pat me on the back or offer encouraging words. It's only when Moose leans over and tells me we need to go, that I actually comprehend how completely I let myself fall apart....and how deeply embedded Emma still is inside my heart.

+++++++++++++++++++++

Moose stays with me that night; flat out telling me that he doesn't trust me enough not to fall off the wagon. He also tells me how much he loves me, how much he values our friendship, and how important I am in his life.

Moose has been to therapy with me a time or two, same as Grace has.

We hang out and play video games for a while, then I give him the bed because there's no way in hell that he's ever going to sleep on my small couch. I leave the T.V. on for noise...for companionship...and to help drown out the voices that are screaming at me to call her. When I eventually fall asleep, it's almost dawn and my dreams are scattered; visions of Faith and Emma intermixed with folks from my meeting.

In the morning, Moose takes off early to get ready for the wedding, and I head to another meeting. Back home, I'm relaxed and once again focused on my plan; gobble down some food, straighten up the house and get myself into my monkey suit. I'm a groomsman, which means I basically have to show up and stand next to Moose and Ryan. Luckily, because the wedding is at the beach and not a church, the formal wear is pretty relaxed; suit jackets, linen slacks, and open collar shirts. Grace has given us the option of going barefoot like she is, but Ryan and I have declined. It's weird if you ask me, but that's my sister for ya.

We congregate as a group in the small parking lot at the beach they've chosen. Typical Grace; she's foregoing all the normal superstitions and is standing there talking to Dad and Ruth, holding tightly to Ryan's hand. Glancing down at the beach, I see the white chairs lined up on either side of the makeshift aisle facing the ocean. Grace has informed me numerous times that she didn't want to waste money on flowers or unnecessary decorations, so it's a very informal event; just what I'd expect from my no-nonsense sister and her equally down to earth, soon-to-be groom.

Ruth shoos all of us except Grace and Dad down onto the beach as people start to arrive and pulls Grace by the hand into their R.V. before anyone can see her. I try chatting with Ryan, but he's pretty green around the gills and letting the nerves get the best of him. Moose, on the other hand, is doing his best to keep Emma entertained and as far away from me as possible.

She looks breathtaking in her knee-length halter dress; the vivid green material a good contrast to her olive skin and dark hair. I wonder if she realizes that her dress is that color because of Faith, or that the pink ribbon tied around Grace's waist is for her too. Green because it was Faith's favorite color, pink as a show of support for breast cancer; two small ways that Grace could include her in this special day even though she's no longer with us. It still gives me a hard stab of sadness right in the heart; all these things that she's missing and will continue to miss out on as the years pass by. I wonder if it will always be like that. Somehow, I think it will; us making memories without her and wondering what it would have been like if she were still here.

I greet people as they start to arrive; folks I remember from Grace's job at the cell phone company and some family members from out of town. Ryan introduces me to his Uncle Joe, the guy who they live next door to. I vaguely remember Grace telling me about his crazy wife and his nightly need to smoke pot in his dark garage. Thankfully, he's alone today, and although he seems like a decent guy I can sure do without the pervy glances he's sending in Emma's direction.

The minister/priest/officiate arrives and gives us a few last minute instructions, and then we take our places just as Ruth arrives to stand next to Emma. A lone musician plays the cello; Grace's cue to start down the short flight of stairs with Dad holding tightly to her arm.

She's gorgeous is her long white gown; the halter style top exactly like Emma's. It's the first time that I realize how alike they are and except for the eye color they could be sisters. They are both petite, although Emma is just a few inches shorter than Grace. Grace's hair is piled on her head, cascading down into a mass of wild curls that wave in the soft breeze. She's bubbling over with happiness and although I'm elated for her, I can't dismiss the sharp stab of jealousy that hits me directly in the center of my chest.

I half-listen as they exchange vows, exchange rings…exchange a kiss as man and wife. Then we're all applauding, most of the women (and Moose) are crying, and Grace is looking up at Ryan like he's her whole world.

Emma once looked at me like that, and now she can't bring herself to look at me at all. It's a sobering thought, and one that steals the breath from my lungs and makes me feel slightly dizzy. For all the happiness that surrounds us today, it's nothing more than salt into an ever-festering wound for her and me. I can only hope we can get through the rest of the night unscathed, and I can send her on her way toward a happy life, free from the burden of my problems.

Our entire group heads back up the stairs toward the parking lot, to the restaurant where the reception is being held. It's a small place, closed for our party only, and boasts an amazing menu and a large outdoor patio for dancing. Moose and Emma head straight for the bar, while I hang back with Dad and Ruth, find a table and settle in our chairs. Once again, I half listen to the chatter around me; I'm too fixated on the churning need in my gut to drink…to run….to hold Emma in my arms and never let her go.

All in all it ends up being a great night, once I'm able to chill out and get out of my head for a while. The food is fantastic, the music is jamming and the crowd is enthusiastic; all great distractions for me. I dance with some of the ladies from Grace's work, with Grace a few times and Ruth too, and even with one of the waitresses, who has made it very clear she'd gladly go home with me if I just ask. I gently let her down and send her on her way; the new me slightly nauseated by the thought of some stranger touching me.

I try not to be the stalker that I feel like I am, but my eyes keep getting drawn to Emma; to her vibrant smile, her laughter with Moose, her whispering back and forth with Grace when they dance together. Getting her alone is going to be a challenge, but my list taunts me from deep in my pocket; reminding me that I've been working my way toward this day for months now and this will be the only the chance I have to make things right.

I finally manage to catch her on her return from the ladies room, call out her name and stop her in her tracks before she can return to the group on the dance floor. She stares at me with that blank expression she's worn since yesterday and immediately averts her eyes when I step close.

"Emma, can I talk to you for a minute?"

Her dark head shakes back and forth. "Now is really not a good time."

"I promise this won't take long." I pull the sheet of paper from my back pocket; keep my eyes centered on it even though I really want to stare into her eyes and beg for forgiveness. "I need to say that I'm sorry."

"Liam…please…not now…"

"I need to do this Em." I know I'm pushing her, which Paul urged me repeatedly not to do. I know only that this is my last chance…my only chance really….to try to make her understand why I did the things I did.

She sighs heavily and pulls her arms across her chest defensively. "Fine."

"I'm sorry that I lied to you about Faith and about how much I thought about her all the time when I was with you." I breathe deep a few times, gather strength and continue on down my list. "I'm sorry I wasn't honest with you, about her, and about lots of other things. I'm sorry I didn't tell you I was still struggling with her death and how much I used alcohol to numb the pain. I'm sorry that I never met your family and I didn't because I was afraid; because that would mean we were getting closer, closer than I'd been with anyone since Faith. And that scared me. Plain and simple." I run my hand through my hair and grip my neck. "I didn't let you stay at my house because I was unable to separate my feelings between you and Faith." I risk a glance at her, see that she's biting on her bottom lip and staring down at her feet. "I'm sorry that I didn't trust you enough to tell you what was going on inside my crazy head. If I had, I truly believe that things might be different." My stomach is one big rolling knot of fear and worry. "I'm sorry I didn't say I love you when you said it to me. I was incapable of loving you the way I should have; the way I could have."

"Please stop," she whispers.

"I'm almost done." I blow out another shaky breath. "I'm sorry for every rotten, shitty, crappy, awful thing I ever did to hurt you. You were the best thing that ever happened to me and I will regret losing you for the rest of my life." I raise my tear-filled eyes to hers; shocked that she's actually willing to look at me. "Thank you for listening to me Em. Take care of yourself. And please be happy."

I turn and walk away before I can drag her into my arms or collapse in a messy heap at her feet. I head directly to my sister, hug her tightly and tell her I need to leave. We exchange a few silent words and she says, "I love you Liam," before sending me on my way.

Then I'm in the truck, and yeah, I'm probably running; but it's either that or stay behind and risk upsetting my sister's big day. The tearing need to find the closest bar and try to drink myself back to normal is like a lasso surrounding my entire body that just tightens slowly around me with each passing minute. A few miles down the road, I pull over, dial my sponsor and once he answers I finally fall completely apart.

I've officially made all my amends. I wish I could say that I felt better now that I've apologized to her, but I feel like there's more I need to say. I'm not going to get that chance....ever....so I need to be grateful that she gave me the few minutes that she did. I need to be grateful I had the chance at all. Now all I have to do is work on making peace with the loss of her; something that took me many, many years to do with Faith.

After my call, I just drive around; listening to music and feeling mostly numb from all the events of the day. I eventually pull up in front of the café; the small light from over the counter barely lighting the space. Not much has changed since I was last here; although I do see that she added a curtain to shield the front counter from the kitchen and installed some new shelves behind the pastry case. It feels like a lifetime since I walked through the door, this place that was once my home away from home; my once new beginning.

My phone buzzes in my pocket and Grace's face lights up the screen. "Hey, what's up?"

"You okay?" I can hear music in the background, a clear indication that the party is still in full swing.

"Yep. Called my sponsor. I'm good."

"Em is a mess. What did you say to her?"

I swear loudly and slump against the café wall. "I told her I was sorry, for everything."

"Made your amends with her then?"

"I did, yes." I don't tell her that there are probably a hundred other things I still need to apologize to her for.

"Good for you Liam."

"I'm sorry I had to do it at your reception Grace. I figured it was the last time I'd ever see her." My throat locks up as I speak the words; tears immediately filling my eyes and racing in streams down my face. "Ah Christ, I need to go."

"You're not gonna drink are you?" I can hear the panic in her voice.

"No Grace, I'm not gonna drink. I'm gonna cry like a big fucking baby." I take a few breaths, get myself semi-under control. "Have a beautiful honeymoon. I love you."

"Love you too Liam."

With one more glance through the café window, I climb into the truck and head for home. Once there, I flick on every light, toss my jacket onto the couch and head into the kitchen to brew a pot of coffee. Thirty minutes later I'm out of my monkey suit, clicking through the channels and half-tempted to watch some porn to take the edge off of the need that's been nagging at me since I laid eyes on Emma last night for the first time.

Christ, she's so beautiful…so enticing….and the fact that she's oblivious to it makes her all the more intriguing and sexy. My mind travels back to that first time with her, up against the wall in the kitchen; her dark eyes wide as she watched intently as I slid into her again and again. I'm rock hard just thinking about it and more than tempted to reach down and finish the job; use the memory as the fantasy I need to find some relief. Then the doorbell peels loudly and I curse under my breath and adjust my jeans; get to my feet and pull the door open.

Moose is standing on the porch, looking at me with an odd expression. "Hey man. How's it goin'?"

I shrug, step back to let him in and once he moves out of the way I see Emma standing right behind him; eyes uncertain, face pale. I'm shocked, caught off guard that she's actually standing at my door. "Uh…hey Em. Come on in." She says nothing as she moves into the house; her dark eyes accessing the space completely. "What are you guys up to?"

Moose rubs his bald head and looks sideways at her before saying, "Uh…Em wanted to talk to you. So I told her I'd bring her over here."

I can't help but laugh at this enormous man who is so visibly uncomfortable. "So what are you? The chaperone?"

He chortles, smacks me hard on the back. "Yeah, right!" His eyes dart to Emma. "I'm not staying."

Emma starts to protest. "Yeah, but you said…."

Moose stares down at her; his huge form towering over her much smaller one. "You've got this gorgeous." He drops a kiss on her head and slaps me once more. "I'm a phone call away if you guys need me." He's gone before either of us can protest.

Then I'm alone with her, feeling grateful and unsettled and more uncertain than I've felt in years. "Have a seat. Want some coffee?"

She nods, sitting uneasily on the edge of the couch. "Sure. Thanks."

When I return, I hand over her cup and take a seat in one of the two chairs, making a conscious effort to keep a good distance between us and not scare her. "So, Moose said you wanted to talk to me."

She nods again, but refuses to look up. "Um…yeah. I've got a few questions if that's all right."

"Of course. Anything."

Her silence shouts loudly into the large room. I watch closely as she opens her mouth, then immediately shuts it again; like she's biting back what she wants to say….or choosing her words very carefully. Eventually, she takes a deep breath, grips her cup until her knuckles turn white, then says, "You spent time in the hospital. Right?"

"Yep. Alcohol poisoning. Almost killed me." That I can make a statement like this speaks volumes to my recovery. A year ago I would never even have admitted to alcohol being an issue; and now I'm blabbing loudly about how immensely it once over-powered my life.

Her head bobs up and down and she takes a sip of coffee. "Have you gotten help for your drinking?"

I nod. "Yes. I went to rehab for a month, and now I'm in Alcoholics Anonymous and go to meetings almost every day. I also see a therapist." The fact that she knows none of this is testament to how tight my friends and family are to me, to my dirty little secrets; and it gives me one more thing to be grateful for. I've always wanted to be the one to tell her what happened to me…and how I'm working to fix all of it one step at a time.

"I didn't realize it was that bad," she says softly, finally raising her head and looking right at me.

"Neither did I. Denial is a big part of it." I hope that I can eventually tell her that I denied so many things….how much I needed help, that I even had a problem, and that my feelings for her were so much more than I ever acknowledged.

She nods. "Are you working?"

"Yeah. Big projects, lots of hours. You know how it is." I feel like I need to bite back that last sentence, then remember what Paul always tells me; always tell the truth and do not censor myself.

"I like your new place," she comments, glancing around again.

I smile at her. "Quite an improvement from the hell hole I was in."

She smiles in return. "Gotta agree with you there." She gets to her feet, wanders around the room, looking at the few framed pictures I have displayed; me and Grace, me and my dad, my favorite one of Faith at the lake. Then I watch as she moves toward the far wall, to the large frame that Grace made for me; watch intently as she looks at each picture and reads each message.

I get to my feet and walk toward her, stop when I'm standing by her side, but not nearly as close as I want to be. I know that I have to give her a wide birth where I'm concerned; crowding or pushing her will only drive her further away. "Grace gave me this as a housewarming gift. These were messages Faith left for me. I found them for the first time that night you came to my apartment."

She gasps and her eyes shoot up to mine. "No wonder you were so...." Wary eyes shoot up to mine and she bites down hard on her lower lip with uncertainty.

"Out of control...distraught....rude as hell?"

She blinks rapidly, a clear sign she's stunned at my honesty. "Yeah. This explains a lot."

I shrug. "But it doesn't explain why I was silent, why I had nothing to say to you when you begged me to, or why I treated you like you didn't matter to me."

"Yeah, but Liam you were upset..."

"Don't make excuses for the way I treated you Emma!" I snap, turning away from her and heading into the kitchen to splash water on my face. Once the anger subsides, I take two spoons out of the drawer and the tub of rocky road out the freezer and head back into the living room.

I hand her a spoon and when she lifts an eyebrow I state, "Peace offering."

"Ah. Okay."

We sit there together, watching some rerun of an old 70's show, chowing down on the ice cream and saying nothing. Just being with her makes me feel good, makes me feel normal…and a whole lot less like the crazy man I've been for the past months without her.

"How are your folks?" I inquire, shoving a huge bite into my mouth.

"Good. My mom asks about you all the time. She wonders how you are." It's my turn for the quizzical expression and she just shrugs nonchalantly. "I talked about you a lot. She feels like she knows you."

I flinch at the knowledge that her mom knows what a dick I've been to her daughter. "And Mario?"

She starts to laugh. "He's stressing. Josie is pregnant again. With twins this time."

"That's great Em."

"Yeah, it really is."

Another few long minutes of silence, then, "I went by the café tonight. It looks really good."

A look of surprise lights her face. "Really? I'm glad you did." Then she starts to talk like she used to; alive with animation, all big brown eyes and wavy, Italian hands, telling me stories about the café, the customers, and the new recipes that she and Grace are working on. She chatters non-stop for a good ten minutes before finally winding down.

"How's it working out with you and Grace?"

She grins at me; digs out a hefty portion of ice cream. "So good. She's a really hard worker, super enthusiastic, and so damn smart it's really scary."

I laugh. "That's really good. It's great to see her so happy, and to have a good friend by her side again."

The smile slides from her face. "Is therapy helping you…with the Faith stuff, I mean?"

Throwing my spoon down on the coffee table, I lean back against the couch and stare up at the ceiling. "Yeah. Like all the other stuff, it's a work in progress. But I've found a certain peace about it, which is a start at least."

"That's really good Liam," she says softly.

Rolling my eyes to the side, I watch as she twirls her empty spoon in her hand; the tension and uncertainty still clearly visible in the stiff way she's sitting just on the edge of the couch…like at any minute she's gonna bolt. It makes me wonder what her trigger will be; more talk about Faith, more talk about what we once were.

She glances over at me, sees me looking at her intently and scoots a little further away. "Um…the wedding was nice."

I hate that I'm disappointed by her change in subject; hate that I'd wish she'd yell….scream at me…throw things around the room. Something, anything, other than this calm acceptance that she seems to have mastered during our months apart.

"Yeah, it was."

She looks at me briefly, then gathers up our spoons and the empty container and heads into the kitchen. I hear her moving around behind me, but I force myself not to look at her; give her the space she obviously needs.

"I'm gonna go. Thanks for the ice cream."

Getting to my feet, I ask, "I thought Moose brought you."

She shakes her head. "No, I followed him here."

"Ah." I'm pretty pissed at this revelation. I was looking forward to extending our time together by driving her home.

Emma pulls open the door, takes a step out and turns back to face me. "Thanks for answering my questions."

"Anytime Em. You know where to find me." I need to make sure she knows I'm still available to her; even if she is locked up tight against me.

"Yeah, well take care of yourself," she states.

"You too. And Em?" I wait until she finally lifts her eyes to mine. "Thank you for listening tonight. It means a lot to me."

She nods. "Night Liam."

I watch her move toward the car, get in and back out without once looking in my direction. Once she's gone, I head inside; lock up for the night and move slowly up the stairs.

I wonder what she'd think if she saw the pictures that I keep up here in my bedroom; pictures of us together at the café, flour all over her face like usual. There are a few pictures from our trip to Monterey, one I took of her and Grace one night at dinner, and my favorite photo, which is next to my bed. I'd taken it early one morning, when the summer sun was streaming into the room, casting shadows across her face. Her long dark hair is splayed over the pillow, hands resting together under her chin; the ethereal beauty of her face in sleep captured with one snap of the camera. What the image doesn't show is how she raised those sleepy eyes to me, smiled warmly, and shoved the sheet down to reveal her naked body to my eyes; gathering me in her arms and welcoming me into her warmth.

Like always, the photo takes my breath away; and simultaneously fills me with sadness and regret. This is the true embodiment of her; the open, welcoming, warm girl who I managed to crush slowly with my dishonesty and lack of trust. I can only be grateful that we had that moment…lots of moments actually….and I'll have those memories to keep me warm at night for years to come.

I wish I could ask her what she's thinking. I wish I could ask her if my hurried apologies at the reception meant anything. I wish I could ask if she's willing to give me a second chance. I wish I could go back a year…. not be the person I was then….and love her like she deserves to be loved; with my whole self, my whole heart. With all of myself….completely hers…forever.

CHAPTER 15

I spend the entire next day staring at my phone; hoping it will ring...and waiting for the doorbell to peel even though I know there's not a hope in hell that it will. I'm not really sure why I think she's going to contact me; it's not like she gave me any indication that our one night of conversation was going to be the first of many.

One week later, I'm no longer checking my phone. I'm certain things are resolved, at least in her head anyway. Me on the other hand, I'm more confused than ever. Meetings help some, but my craving now is not the bottle, but answers. I want to know what she's thinking and if she considers us over for good. I have lots of questions....more each day....but mostly I just really need to see her; need to look into those big brown eyes and see the truth that she's always been unable to hide from me. Up until recently, that is.

Moose checks in at the end of the week; wants to know if I want to hang out, maybe get some pizza. I'm chomping at the bit for something to take my mind off of Emma and my endless hours of over-thinking and wondering, so I immediately agree. Minutes later I'm in my truck and headed toward what I pray will be a few hours of peace. Emma-free peace at that.

As usual, Moose is late; and I spend that time alone sitting at the table, drinking iced tea and once again thinking about her. When he finally walks through the door I'm shocked to see Emma by his side; and silently I wonder if all my obsessing about her has somehow brought her here. It's dumb, I know.

"Hey man," he says, greeting me with his usual back slap.

I give him a head nod and turn my attention to the hesitant girl behind him. "Hi Em. This is a nice surprise." Her eyes dart around, she chews on her lip and lifts hesitant eyes to Moose. My stomach slides up into my throat as I realize my mistake; she's not here for me....he just didn't tell her I'd be here.

Moose settles his massive frame on the bench seat across from me, leaving no space for Emma. He starts chatting away like usual and I pretend like I'm listening while I slide over and give her as much space next to me as possible. She sits stiffly on the edge of the bench, gripping her purse tightly in her lap.

"So, did ya order?" Moose asks.

I shake my head. "Waiting on you."

He gets to his feet. "I'll get it. Whatcha drinking gorgeous?" She says something softly to him and he heads off to the order window.

The silence is deafening. I don't dare look at her for fear she'll jump up and run, or just start screaming accusations at me. I'm sure she's assuming that I had something to do with this forced meeting, and I can't imagine how desperate I must look in her eyes.

I give it a few long minutes, then I glance over at her and say, "I'm really sorry about this Em. I had no idea what he was up to. I hope you can believe that." It's the best I can do under these circumstances and I secretly can't wait to get Moose alone and ream him a new one.

She shrugs, looking everywhere but right at me. "I won't be staying."

"I'll go," I state. "You have fun with Moose."

"Yeah, so I got an extra-large supreme," Moose announces, handing her a soda and resuming his seat across from us. "Liam, have you heard from Gracie?"

His interruption has somehow halted either one of us from leaving, though she's still sitting there poised like she's preparing for battle. "No. She's on her honeymoon. Why would she call me?"

He shrugs. "To make sure you're okay, I guess."

I glare at him. "I'm fine Moose. Let it go."

He ignores me and directs his next question to Emma. "So, how's business?"

"Good. Busy."

"Dude, have you tried those tube things she makes? They're filled with some kinda crazy filling that gets me hard every time I eat one. Fuck, they're amazing."

I can't help but laugh at his antics, and his spot-on description of my favorite pastry. "Uh, yeah, they are amazing." I risk a glance at Emma, see that she too is snickering; her fingers finally starting to unclench on her bag. "And they're called cannoli."

Moose rolls his eyes at me. "Whatever dude. I don't give a fuck what they're called. I just want to eat like a dozen, starting now."

Emma is laughing loudly. "We'll stop by the café after we're done here and I'll send you home with some."

"Fuck yeah!" he grins.

Jealousy streaks through me, hard and fast. I don't want him eating her pastries, driving her around or spending time with her. I'm supposed to be doing that; I'm supposed to be helping her out in the kitchen, then fucking her senseless after the shop is closed.

Not anymore, my obnoxious subconscious reminds me. *You lost that chance months ago asshole.*

Our pizza arrives and Moose immediately dives in; consuming a huge piece before Emma and I can even take a few bites. My appetite is gone; taken away completely by the images that are now filling my head.... images of Moose permanently taking my place alongside her. For the first time in a long time, the thought of alcohol makes me sick; the need to lash out, hit something...hit him...is what's burning inside me now.

I somehow manage to make it through the rest of our evening together; although by the time we eventually walk out to our trucks I'm seriously seeing red. Moose gives me his token back slap and I offer up a goodbye to the two of them, get in my truck and head home without a backwards glance.

My dreams are haunting that night, waking me from a deep sleep with the images of Emma and Moose together in bed. I hate that I'm feeling this resentful of the friend who has taken such good care of me during the past tough months; hate that I can't just be happy for him and hope that he does a better job of loving her than I did.

But the idea of them together makes me sick; makes me physically ill to think about her screaming out his name instead of mine. I'm a selfish ass to believe I'd be the last name on her lips, the last one making her scream with pleasure. Just the thought of another guy....any guy....touching her makes my head spin out of control. And yet I just have to listen to the voice in my head, the one nagging at me that I did this...I drove her away....I'm the reason she's gone....to snap me back to reality.

Tossing back the covers, I head downstairs and start the coffee; the clock on the stove tells me that it's inhumane to be up at this hour. Clicking on the T.V., I settle in the middle of the couch and try to lose myself in some random repeat.

Three hours later there's a knock at my door. I'm blurry eyed, shaky from the pot of coffee that I've consumed, and still royally pissed off at my best friend. Yanking open the door, I'm stunned to see Emma standing there. She's dressed for the café; the tight purple tee and jeans like a taunt for my empty hands.

"Morning," she says. "Did I wake you?"

I shake my head and take a step back to let her in. "No. I've been up for a while."

She hands me a white paper bag. "I thought I'd bring you some cannoli."

Her sweet gesture speaks volumes, but I'm hesitant to assume she means anything by this early morning call. "Thanks Em. Can I get you some coffee?"

She glances down at her watch. "Sure. I have a little time before I need to be back." She follows me into the kitchen, silently watching as I pour her coffee; add the splash of milk that I know she prefers.

I hold up the bag. "Want to share?"

"Sure."

Once we're seated on the couch, plates of mouth-watering cannoli in our hands, I glance over at her and state, "I'm sorry about last night. I'm pretty pissed at Moose."

She shrugs. "Yeah, I was too." I feel her grin right in the pit of my stomach. "I only gave him two cannoli because of it."

"Can I ask you something?" The question has been eating at me since last night. When she nods in agreement, I rush forward, "Are you and Moose together now?"

Emma frowns. "Together? Like as a couple?"

"Yeah."

She slams her plate down on the table and gets to her feet. "No Liam. I'm not with him. I'm not with anyone." She walks across the room, giving herself distance and space from me. "I couldn't be with anyone even if I wanted to."

"Come again?"

She swears loudly and pulls her arms across her chest. "Never mind. Just forget it."

Getting to my feet, I move slowly to her. "No. Tell me what you mean."

Her eyes are dark, hard and unfeeling and very much pissed off at me. "You're such an ass Liam. Are you really that dense?"

Now I'm the one who is pissed. "What the fuck are you talking about?"

She throws her hands up. "Do you know how much it hurts to have you ask me if I'm with someone else?"

Confounded, I'm mumble, "Uh…no."

"Well it does. It makes me think you have no idea how invested I was in you. How you think I could just so easily go into another relationship so quickly after us." She lifts a brow. "Is that what you've done? Are you with someone new?"

"Fuck no!" I snap. "Why would I do that when you're the only one I want to be with?"

"Exactly," she whispers.

Every emotion that I've felt in the past week rolls right through my body. "What are you saying Em?"

Her eyes find mine. "I'm saying that the idea of being with anyone else makes me sick." She takes a step back, putting distance between us again and effectively putting me in my place; her silent way of telling me not to jump the gun.

"I know what you mean," I reply. I move back to the couch, mostly because my legs feel shaky and I'm overwhelmed with the need to touch her.

"I'd like to try to be your friend again Liam."

Anger surges to the surface. I know exactly what she's saying, sticking me in the fucking friend zone. And although I loathe the idea of being only that to her, at least I'd be something; and that's a hell of a lot more than the nothing I've been lately. "Me too Em."

"I'm not making any promises," she cautions.

"Me neither." The warning voices are back; loud and nagging in the back of my head, reminding me that I've been cautioned…many times… on getting involved with someone while I'm still in the middle of my recovery.

She joins me back on the couch, picks up her plate and starts munching on the cannoli; completely unmoved by the fact that she's shoved me off my foundation and caught me totally by surprise with her friend request.

We sit there together, sipping coffee and eating her amazing cannoli; Magnum PI keeping us company and helping to stifle the awkward silence that seems to easily settle between us. When our plates are empty, she gathers everything together and heads into the kitchen, then immediately walks straight for the door. "I've gotta get to the café. Have a good day." She glances at me briefly over her shoulder.

I remain seated, giving her the space she needs; ensuring her a quick getaway. "Yeah, you too. And Em, thanks for coming by."

She turns slightly and throws me a wide smile. "You bet. See you soon."

Like the idiot I am, I just sit there staring at the closed front door, like I actually think she might walk back in and declare her undying love for me. That nasty little voice in my head reminds me loudly that I should be lucky that she wants to build a friendship again; she could be walking away for good. The nasty voice also reminds me...very loudly, I might add....that long ago she did declare her love for me; and all I did was remain silent.

Picking up my phone, I scroll through it until I find my list of meetings; shove my shoes on and grab my keys. A meeting is exactly what I need to get my feet under me again; exactly what will help put my life back into perspective and remind me where my priorities have to be.

++++++++++++++++++++

By the time Faith's birthday rolls around a few weeks later, I'm convinced that Emma's 'friend' declaration was nothing more than a rouse. I've not heard from her since she walked out my door that morning, and since I'm unsure exactly what the parameters are of this so-called friendship, I have no intention of being the first to call; not until I have a clear understanding of exactly what she wants from me.

My therapist has encouraged me to make these birthdays and anniversaries a positive day, instead of spending so much time dwelling on what won't be happening for Faith. "Celebrate her," he said to me last week. "Celebrate her life, even though it was short lived. Celebrate that you knew her and that you loved her. Not everyone can say that about someone."

I know he's right. I have spent too much time these past years not celebrating and focusing solely on what I've....what we've....lost. A few years ago Grace threw a birthday party to celebrate Faith, and even though I spent the entire next day drinking away my life, it felt good at the time to remember her in a positive way.

I read my vows to her that day; revealed to the group of friends and family the words I'd written years before, but was never allowed to actually say to her until after she died. I still have them, tucked into an envelope in my box of keepsakes from our time together. I've also kept an old diary of hers that her mom gave to me; words she'd written about us, about her long-ago teenage crush on me; the repeated scribbling of what would have been her married name written all over the inside cover.

Faith Mathers

Mrs. Faith Mathers

Mrs. Liam Mathers

I think about that now, about the other things I have; old love letters we exchanged, the first stuffed animal I bought for her….and I am sad…. but I'm also so very, very grateful. Not many people I know are as lucky as I am; I knew without a shadow of a doubt how much she loved me. And even though she's gone, I have tangible, written proof of her commitment to me, to us. I'll always be thankful knowing a part of her will always be with me; even if it's just a long ago teenage fantasy or words written when our relationship was first blooming.

I decide to spend her birthday doing what I'd normally do; go to work, go to a meeting and come home. Once there, I head straight to my room and pull out the box of stashed memories; read through the vows and the diary, thumb through all the mementoes. Then I decide that I'm going to start a new tradition. Every year on her birthday I'm going to write to her….tell her what's going on in my life, how I'm feeling, what I've been going through. That way, when I'm old and gray I can go back and read through them, just as I'm reading through her diary now, and I can be grateful I remembered so much about her.

I write for well over an hour, then seal the letter up in an envelope, write the date on the outside and drop it in the box. I'm proud of myself for how I've handled this day, but still relieved that it will soon be over and I can let her rest for another few months; until October rolls around and I'll be forced to deal with it again.

One day at a time, I remind myself. One day at a time.

My phone buzzes loudly and I pick it up without looking at the screen. "Yeah?"

"Hi Liam, its Emma."

I want to laugh; it's not like I am ever going to forget the sound of her voice. "Hey Em. I'm glad you called."

"I just wanted to see….um….well….." She stops talking and I hear her breathe in and out a few times. "I j-just….well…uh…."

"It's okay. Take your time." I prop myself up against the pillows and kick my shoes off.

A few long, silent moments go by, then she says softly, "Um…well I know what today is and I just wanted to see if you were doing okay."

Once more, she's caught me off guard and I'm left speechless. I'm sure Grace…or maybe Moose…told her about today, but I'm shocked that she's putting herself out there on a day like this; doing it for me, which is even more unsettling. "Yeah Em, I'm good. I'm really concentrating on thinking about her in a positive way, and not dwelling on the bad stuff."

"Good for you," she replies.

"I decided to write her a letter, just tell her stuff that's going on in my life."

"And did it help at all?"

A smile drifts over my face. "You know, I think it did."

"I'm glad. Really I am."

I glance over at the nightstand; at the 5 x 7 picture of us taken in Monterey. My mind drifts back…her dark hair spread over the white sheet….our reflections in the bathroom mirror….those whispered words 'I love you'. I'd give anything to be back there with her now; do things differently, not hide from her or run from the truth. I'd give anything to have her small fingers digging in my back, her pleading words in my ear, her mouth on mine. I know it's all gone now, but the fantasy is vivid and all-too real; especially with her voice on the other end of the phone.

"I miss you." My words are barely audible, whispered through gritted teeth; my eyes centered on her face in the photo before me.

"I miss you too," she whispers. "Bye Liam."

"Bye Em. Thanks for calling."

After I end the call, I toss the phone across the bed, get to my feet and strip off my clothes. The frigid water pelts down on my body, though it does nothing for the need that her brief phone call lit up inside me. Reaching down, I wrap my fist around my ridged length and let myself fall slowly into the fantasy; my mouth trailing down her body, between her legs….our bodies sliding together so perfectly. She's begging, scratching my back, pleading with me not to stop; the hot, slick warmth of her body welcoming me in. I stroke faster, mimic the fantasy; my body thrusting into hers until she's screaming out my name. I come hard; my groan echoing off the tile walls, the water pelting my sensitive flesh.

Panting, I lean forward, let the spray soak me completely and wash away the erotic fantasy. The release is welcome, and much needed after all these long months alone. But my self-gratification does nothing for the need that still pulses inside me; the need I have to make her mine again. Tonight is sure a great way to start, and the first encouraging step I feel we've taken. I know we have a long way to go, but her simple last words to me are all I need to give me some hope that maybe…just maybe….she can be mine again.

+++++++++++++++++++++

A few weeks later I'm invited to a birthday barbeque for Grace. Right off, she tells me that Emma is going to be there and I'm gonna have to suck it up and deal with it. I'm not sure where all my sister's sudden kick-ass attitude is coming from, especially concerning me and Emma and the history between us. I guess this is her way of keeping us both in her life, without dancing around the past. What she doesn't know is that Emma and I have been talking….somewhat….during the past few weeks, and I'm fairly certain we're past the awkward stage that was so apparent at the wedding.

It started when I sent her a message the day after we spoke; thanking her for her call. We chatted back and forth a few times and then I didn't hear from her for almost a week. Then she called and we talked about normal stuff for a few minutes, just as we used to do. Since then, we've pretty much exchanged texts every few days.

I arrive late to the party because of work, and the gang is laughing and drinking, sitting outside on lawn chairs. Moose is there with his on-again girlfriend Autumn and as usual he greets me with a hard back slap.

"Hey brother, how's it goin'?" He asks, bouncing Autumn on his left knee like a child. She's about the size of one, so I suppose it's appropriate.

"Good man." I take the empty seat, which just happens to be right next to Emma. "Hey Em. Good to see you." She's shockingly beautiful in a pair of white denim shorts and a red halter top; that mass of silky hair pulled up into a high ponytail, leaving her tantalizing neck way too exposed for my liking. All kinds of ideas float through my head, starting and ending with my lips on her soft skin.

She grins at me. "Good to see you too. How was work?"

I rattle on about the job we're currently working on, my eyes locked on hers the entire time. I don't dare look down, where the deep V of her shirt dips low and far too enticing, reminding me all too vividly what lies beneath. As usual, she has no idea how incredibly tempting she looks, or how much my blood heats just looking at her.

Ryan cooks burgers for all of us and once we're seated again with food in hand Emma and I start right back up, talking about life in general like we used to do. It was one of the things I used to like best about her...and still do....her ability to just enjoy the normalcy of life. She's not the kind-of gal who needs to have plans every night, or a super exciting social life, and I guess that's because she has such a rich family history and is clear in her devotion toward making the café her life. She has a certain peace about her, a humble way of moving through life and just enjoying the simple things. It's something I've always admired.

Emma and I chat with Moose and Autumn, although they spend a considerable amount of time swapping spit and making the two of us feel uncomfortable. Grace and Emma give me updates from the café, Ryan talks about the new tattoo he's working on for a buddy of his, and overall it's just a nice, normal evening; so far and apart from what I'm used to with my drunken binges of late.

When the evening ends I walk Emma to her car; the balmy June night sky alight with thousands of stars and a full moon. "You working tomorrow?" she asks, turning to me and leaning against the car door.

I shake my head. "No. Thank God."

"You should come by the café. I just made cannoli."

Grinning, I reply, "Oh, I'll be there." My eyes lock on hers briefly, then I can't resist the temptation to dip them lower; take in the tempting slope of her breasts peeking out from the revealing shirt, the hint of her tan, flat stomach. "Christ you're so beautiful," I whisper.

Her hand snakes out, fingertips touch mine; a touch I feel, like usual, just where I shouldn't. "Don't say things like that. You make it hard for me to walk away."

"Then don't," I reply, looking directly at her once again. "I want you Em."

"I want you too," she whispers, her eyes widening as I step closer. "But I'm scared."

My hand cups her neck. "I know you are babe. So am I." I lean over, just until our lips almost touch, then whisper, "When you're ready, you know where to find me. I'm not going anywhere." It's much too tempting and although I want to kiss her senseless I force myself to take a step back; pull my hand from hers and extract my keys from my back pocket.

She's clearly unsettled by our closeness; her eyes are dark and filled with need, her breathing is labored, and her nipples are rock hard against the soft cotton material of the halter. I'm certain she has no idea of the amount of restraint I'm showing, when all I really want to do is slam her back against the car and lick every inch of her skin.

"I'll see you tomorrow," I reply, giving myself one long, last look before heading off to my truck. She's still standing against her car door staring at me when I drive away.

+++++++++++++++++++++

Emma

"Hey girl, what are you still doing out here?" Grace calls from the apartment doorway.

I turn and walk across the grass, grumbling, "I need a drink."

Grace knows me well; knows I really don't drink at all…and she also knows I wouldn't ask for one if I wasn't desperate. She nods at me, points to the couch for me to sit, then retrieves a large bottle of tequila and three shot glasses. Ryan gives her a look, like he's uncertain about whether or not he should stay, and she just nods and points to the Lazy Boy.

"All right Em, what happened between you and my brother now?"

I toss back the first shot and hold my glass out for another. "Um, it's kinda embarrassing."

"I can go in the other room," Ryan says.

"Nope. You're staying," Grace replies. "We might need a man's opinion."

He rolls his eyes and tosses back his shot. "Whatever."

Grace glares at him for a second, then looks over at me. "Did you guys argue?"

I laugh. "Not hardly."

"So, tell me. What's wrong, and why is it embarrassing?"

Swearing under my breath, I gulp down the second shot; let it burn down my throat. "Well…um…things got sort of….intense between us."

"You mean he wanted to fuck you?"

My face flames and I risk a glance at Ryan, who seems completely at ease with this whole conversation; though I do notice that he's trying really hard not to snicker. "Um....yeah."

"Did you want to fuck him?"

"God yes." The words are out before I can bite them back, and Grace... bitch that is...just starts to laugh. "Knock it off Grace, it's not funny."

"Yes it is! What are you doing here, talking to us? You should be at his place, screwing each other until you're too tired to even blink."

"Sounds like a good plan to me," Ryan smirks, winking at Grace.

"Shut up, both of you!" I snap, getting to my feet. "I can't sleep with him, not yet. We have too much stuff to work through. And I'm still afraid."

"Afraid of what?" Grace plops down on Ryan's lap, runs her fingers through his short hair and looks at up me with large, curious blue eyes.

"The drinking. All his issues with Faith. His inability to be truthful with me about all of it."

Grace nods. "Those are all valid reasons Em, but he is really working hard to better himself. He goes to meetings every day, he sees his therapist once a week. He's a changed guy."

"Yeah. Sure seems like he is." I lean one hip on the edge of the couch. "Ryan, can I ask what you think?"

He shrugs. "Well, I agree with Grace. I think he's working really hard to be a better person. I think a lot of the reason he's doing it is because of you." His mouth lifts in a knowing grin. "As far as the sex goes, sometimes you just need to work out your shit on each other's bodies. The talking can come after. You know, when you're relaxed."

I roll my eyes at him, then watch as he nuzzles Grace's neck and whispers something in her ear. "Okay you two, I'm outta here. Thanks for the advice."

"Em!" Grace calls, just as I start through the door. "Give Liam a second chance. I promise, you won't regret it. He's a really good guy."

I nod. "I know he is. Thanks."

I'm grateful to my friends for their honesty; and so incredibly jealous of what they have together. I know they've worked really hard to get to this good place, and from what Grace has shared with me they've had to overcome their own hurdles where Faith was concerned. But somehow they've managed to do it; to find a peace about it and make a good life together. I just have to wonder if Liam and I can do that as well.

CHAPTER 16

When I arrive home from Grace's the first thing I do is take a cold shower. I'm practically cross-eyed with my need for Emma, and I know that if I have a hope in hell of acting like a normal person when I see her in the morning, I'm gonna have to pull my shit together.

After pulling on shorts and a tank top, I head back downstairs and dig around in my stash of movies; pull out "The Terminator" and pop it in the DVD player. The movie is a good distraction, but I still find myself zoning out; reliving those few moments by her car, the heat between us exactly like it was all those months ago.

I wonder if she remembers that; the deep, intense need we always had for one another. I wonder if she remembers how it felt to have me touch her, kiss her. I wonder if she...like me...has been unable to get the images of us together out of her head.

Groaning, I blow out a deep breath and will my body not to react to my thoughts. Obsessing about us together as we once were will do me no good. The past is over, and whatever happens now will depend on whether or not she will be able to trust me again and whether or not I can hold my shit together. Until that happens, I'm just going to have to sit back and keep working my program, be patient, and wait for her.

The doorbell peels loudly and for a brief moment I consider that it might be Emma. The hope is quickly dashed by the loud voice screaming in my head reminding me that this is going to take time. Rushing her will only backfire on me.

But when I pull the door open and see her standing on my porch, that voice in my head is quickly silenced. She looks hopeful...slightly nervous....and still a whole lot turned on. Her dark eyes quickly scan me up and down, and I can't help but notice the flush on her cheeks or the way she looks at me like she wants to eat me alive.

"Hey Em," I say, stepping back to let her in. "This is a nice surprise. Everything okay?"

She nods and glances at the T.V. "Am I interrupting?"

"Nope. Have a seat." I watch intently as she ignores my request and moves around the room in a slow, measured pace. "Are you okay?"

Her eyes find mine. "I talked to Grace."

Confused, I frown. "Okay. What did she say?"

"She thinks I should give you a second chance."

My heart thumps loud and fast in my chest. "What do you think?"

"I'm beginning to think she's right." She stops pacing and shoves her hands in the pockets of her shorts, which pulls them down just slightly to reveal that tantalizing strip of her flat belly. I notice how this time she's the one with the wandering eyes; repeatedly scanning my body up and down, effectively stripping me bare just with a look. Then she glances up at me again, and says softly, "Ryan thinks we should just take out our frustrations on each other's bodies. And figure the rest out later."

I'll have to remember to thank Ryan tomorrow. Chuckling, I reply, "I have to agree with him. But what do you think?"

She moves quickly, until she's standing right in front of me and our bare toes are touching. "I think I want you take me upstairs to your bedroom, strip off my clothes, and make love to me until we're too tired to blink."

I grin, raise an eyebrow at her. "You come up with that one all on your own, because it sure sounds like my sister?"

She laughs. "Yeah, it was Grace."

In one quick movement I'm lifting her off her feet and moving toward the stairs, racing up the long flight and not setting her down until she's right at the edge of the bed. I give her minute to look around, see the look of surprise that crosses her face when she sees the picture of us together on the nightstand and the small ones on the dresser; the large one of her sleeping that I just had framed on the wall across from the bed.

"What is all this?" she whispers, reaching for my hand.

My eyes find hers. "This is me, knowing you are the best thing that ever happened to me." I grasp her other hand. "You saved me Em, with your love, your laughter, your friendship. My life has changed completely because of you and I'm so grateful to you for not giving up on me."

Her eyes fill with tears. "But I did Liam. At least for a little while anyway."

I shake my head, gather her in my arms and lean my forehead against hers. "No you didn't babe. You were hurt, and rightly so. But I don't believe you ever gave up on me or on us."

Her smile is wide and bright. "I might have wanted to, but somehow you were always right there in my heart."

We stand there together, just breathing in one another, simply absorbing the reality that the long arduous months apart might actually be over. Her tears eventually stop and its then that I lean over, brush my lips against hers and whisper, "I love you Emma."

Eyes wide in shock, she pulls back slightly. "Really?"

Laughing, I reply, "Of course really. I've probably loved you the entire time, but I was too much of an asshole to admit it."

"Really?" she repeats.

"Yes Em, I love you. I love everything about you; your kindness, your laughter, your amazing beauty." I lean closer and whisper, "Want to know what I love the most?" She nods. "Your tortilla things."

She throws her head back and laughs loudly, though I'm quick to silence it with a kiss. As I peel the clothes from her body, lay her down on my bed and love her thoroughly, I let myself feel it all; the elation, the bittersweet loss of our months apart, the hope for a long future together. I've spent so much time running from everything, that letting myself actually feel something…anything….everything….fills my heart with a sense of euphoria no bottle could ever match.

I'm no fool; I know my struggle with alcohol will be a lifetime challenge. I also know that meetings and therapy will be as much a part of my future as Emma will be. And I'm grateful; for the way the meetings humble me, center me, remind me of who I am and what I've done. I'm grateful for the therapy and the constant reminder that I'll always be a work in progress. I'm most grateful for Emma, for her love, her friendship, and her ability to stick with me even though it's rough and scary and I've given her many reasons to turn and walk away.

"Liam…please…" she begs, looking up at me with those amazing brown eyes.

Loving Emma is the best thing that ever happened to me, and in a way, I'll always be grateful to Faith for that. Faith taught me about love…about friendship…and about commitment. I'll never forget that…never forget her…and I know she'll always be watching, from her perch up above, beer in hand….loving me always.

EPILOGUE

The weather is crisp and sunny this October morning as I drive toward my destination. It's the first time in six years that on this day I've felt nothing but peace. It's taken me a long, long time to get here, but during it all I've learned a boatload about myself. I know there's still a lot of work to do, but I'm sure as hell finally on the right path.

The road winds through large, wrought-iron gates; the acres of land spread out in front of me. Perfectly trimmed grass lies like a soft blanket, and large Oak trees fan out next to one another, a perfect shade for what lies below.

Once I've parked, I take a minute to just look around and take it all in. This will be my final time. I'm here to say goodbye.

"You don't have to do this," Emma whispers from the seat next to me.

My eyes meet hers and I can't help but smile. Strangely enough, she's more nervous than I am. "Yeah babe, I do." I throw open the cab door and slide out. She quickly follows, holding the large bundle of sunflowers that we purchased on our way here. Our eyes lock briefly and the look we share says what no amount of words can. We've come a long way, she and I. I'm a different person now than I was that day long ago, when I sat staring at the coffin in the bright sunshine. I'm different now…better…because of her, and because of what I've been through.

We're silent as we move across the grass hand in hand, carefully avoiding the headstones that are embedded there. Even though I've only been here once, I know exactly where I'm headed. Like many things in my life, this is something I won't soon forget; a memory permanently tattooed in my mind.

Faith's headstone is one of the few in this section that are upright, the words her parents chose so long ago etched into the light grey granite directly under her name:

Always missed, forever loved

No truer words were ever spoken. I will always, always miss Faith. And yes, I will always wish that things had been different; that she wouldn't be gone and wouldn't be missing out on all the crazy and wonderful things that have been happening.

She will be forever loved; by me especially, by her parents, and of course by Grace. And I'm certain there will always be this empty space inside my heart because we lost her, because she was never allowed to live the full and amazing life she should have. Instead we have her memory, our memories of time spent with her that will always be precious and cherished.

"Hello darlin'," I say quietly, brushing stray leaves off the headstone. "I'm sorry it's taken me so long to get here." Glancing down, my eyes meet Emma's; her reassuring warm smile giving me the courage I need to continue.

My eyes travel back down, to this cold, tangible reminder of a short life lived to its fullest. No marker, gravestone, or words will ever perfectly represent what an impact she made on my life. I feel so blessed to have known her and to have called her my friend for so many years. I'm so honored to have loved her....and yes, I can say that in the past tense now without hesitating. She was a gift to us and with her passing we've all discovered new, enlightening and even scary things about ourselves. In a crazy way, Faith would have loved that.

"I miss you Faith. I'll always miss you." Squatting down, I let my fingers trace over her name. "You told me once in one of your picture messages that you wanted me to find love again." Emma's fingers squeeze mine. "And at the time I really believed I could never love anyone but you. I didn't believe that I deserved to find a great love, twice in one lifetime." Leaning forward, I mock whisper. "Wanna hear a secret? I did."

The wind rustles through the leaves of the tree that shades us, and in the distance I hear the soft chirp of bird. Standing upright, I pull Emma close. It might be my imagination, but I swear this is Faith's way of reaching out to me. It would be just like her too....to reach out from that great beyond and give her approval.

"Faith, I want you to meet Emma."

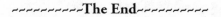

~~~~~~~~~~The End~~~~~~~~~~

ACKNOWLEDGEMENTS

I want to thank my family first and foremost, for encouraging me always. Mark…you are the love of my life and my best friend…you are the reason I've decided to take this chance and dive into the scary world of writing novels. Without your encouragement and faith in me, I never could have taken that first step. Jordan and Tyler…my sweet, amazing, super-smart kids….thank you for supporting me and helping me whenever I asked. Being your mom is my greatest blessing and I'm stunned by the incredible adults you've grown into. You will always be my babies and I am so very, very lucky to be your mom!

I'd like to thank my cheering section: My parents…who tell every person (strangers included) about my books. I love you both…and I'm so grateful for the foundation you've given me. Having you be a part of this second book – helping me with a title, cover, editing or story ideas – just reaffirmed what I've always known….I have the best parents in the world and I'm such a lucky girl!

My baby brother Greg….you read my first book 'Losing Faith', not because you have a great love of romance stories, but because I wrote it. I love you for that…and for so many other things…and I look forward to reading your published works someday soon!

Dee…you got to read this one first, because like me you just can't get enough Liam. Thank you for the free editing, the critiques and ALL the words of encouragement! Deb…your wise, honest words always push me to be better, to do better. Thank you for everything! Randyn…a girl couldn't ask for a better friend, or a more valued social networking/marketing 'assistant'. And to the rest of the gang (you know who you are) …thank you for loving my books, sight unseen…and pimping me out at every turn just to get someone to pick them up and read them. I am so very, very grateful to all of you and I thank each and every one of you for your guidance and for always, always believing in me.

To my amazing mother-in-law Frances…your strength through loss has been an inspiration to us all. Dad would have been so proud of you!

Wes LeRoy from AuthorHouse…you have been my champion since day one. You've fought for me and supported me, even when I was completely frustrated and overwhelmed. I thank you for always being there and giving me a chance to see my dream come true.

I share this book with all the others like me, who've traveled the painful, vast, unknown road of grief. It's a learning lesson for sure, one of the hardest, which goes without saying. I'd especially like to acknowledge the caregivers out there, for doing a thankless job and committing yourself fully to the care of your ailing loved one. Watching someone suffer on a daily basis is most certainly a tragedy, but it is also a great life lesson. More than anything, I believe that you learn the value of friendship and what it means to really and truly love someone selflessly. That's a gift that cannot be denied.

The inspiration and many of the ideas for these two books came from my own experience with my sweet, crazy, wonderful friend Deanna. Sissy… you were our gift and I was so blessed to have had you in my life for as long as I did. I've learned so many things since saying goodbye to you, but more than anything I've learned how incredibly extraordinary friendship can be. Thank you for that. I love you…and miss you…every single day.

Finally, to all the strangers out there, who've taken a chance on my books, liked my Facebook page, or followed me on Twitter.…saying thank you can't properly convey how blessed I feel. Having had this dream all my life, and to know that it's being shared with complete strangers, is overwhelming and humbling. You've embraced my characters and their stories in your heart, and I'll be forever grateful. – AJ

Author Biography

Alexis James lives on the beautiful Central California coast. She married the love of her life and twenty-six years later he can still make her laugh….every single day. Her greatest joy is being a mom to her two children, her family and her writing.

Alexis's love of reading was inspired by her mother. She has proudly passed this love of the written word onto her own daughter. She loves any story that makes you feel…makes you think…and occasionally makes you cry.

Her first novel, "Losing Faith", was released in September 2014 and is available for sale at Amazon and Barnes & Noble.
She invites you to visit her author pages on Facebook and Goodreads, and her website: alexisjamesauthor.wix.com/alexis-james. You can also follow her on Twitter or you can email her at: alexisjamesauthor@gmail.com

Printed in the United States
By Bookmasters